22.47

s

RANDOM
HOUSE

LARGE
PRINT

the life all around me
by Ellen Foster

Kaye Gibbons

+ + +

the life all around me
by Ellen Foster

RANDOM HOUSE
LARGE PRINT

**The Library of Congress has established a
Cataloging-in-Publication record for this title.**

ISBN-13: 978-0-375-72851-8
ISBN-10: 0-375-72851-1

www.randomlargeprint.com

FIRST LARGE PRINT EDITION

10 9 8 7 6 5 4 3 2 1

This Large Print edition published in accord with
the standards of the N.A.V.H.

JAN 17, 2006

For Barbara Sue Atkins Allen Batts
The town lady with all the names,
Who prefers life and fabric textured.
And
For my daughters, Mary, Leslie, and Louise,
Why and how I do this.
And with all thanks to Connie May Fowler,
Who led me to Joy Harris,
Who led me to Ann Patty,
Who led to this, this next one, the one after that . . .

September 20, 1974

President Derek C. Bok
Harvard University
Cambridge, Massachusetts

Dear President Bok,

My name is Ellen Foster. I hope this finds you happy, in good health, and thriving in picturesque New England. It is not quite as scenic here in my part of North Carolina, also known as Variety Vacationland, but this is because I live in the flat, blank section between the Atlantic Ocean and the Great Smokey Mountains, which team up to account for the Variety.

One of my mottoes is that nothing

you think, feel, or do should be watered down, so when I decided to try out for college, Harvard sounded like the only place to be. The main reason I'm returning my information to you instead of the correct office is because there happen to be some things off the average about me and I needed to make sure you know they're reality. Wanting to start Harvard at only fifteen could seem like a tale, for example, but it's true and I believe it makes sound sense because of all the surplus living that was jammed into the years.

My childhood was the kind that saturates you with quick ambition to think through and begin the next episode of your life, although I've been trying to seize each day and appreciate it more as is. A compare and contrast would be trying to break the trend of picking through oranges and handling them until you believe you've finally come across the perfect example to taste.

Those years also made me into an individual who wouldn't be disdone by the large experience of leaving my road to go learn amid ten thousand or so older strangers, not to say anything is currently the matter. Everything has definitely been on the up in up, but even if I was trying to escape pressing hardship at home or a checkered reputation at school, I wouldn't select Harvard to go on the lam.

A person who graduated from there was supposed to grade how close I come to being Harvard material, and I need to let you know I went to town to meet the man we have, but when I got to his nursing home I found him unaware. He'd had another stroke the day before and is now locked in a state of deep coma, but if another one crops up before the deadline, I'll get them to create an opinion and send it to you immediately. The bookmobile librarian who told me about the man is keeping her eyes peeled, but for now, I'd appreciate it if you could please allow this letter to count toward the missing point of view.

If the man had been able to ask why I felt motivated toward Harvard, I would've said I want to be exposed to harder teachers who have strict yet interesting requirements and a student body that thrives on curiosity. It'd be fascinating to be in a lunchroom with people sharing information about simple miracles, such as the smallpox and hookworm vaccinations, or having someone speak up and tell about a family vacation to Crete. In fact, my goal is to study both English and medicine and then enter the field of epidemic disease research. I see myself going into the wilds of places like Bali or Tahiti to research folk customs of medical cures and deliver vaccines as well as lessons on both nutrition and poetry.

To reach this ideal, what I believe I need to do now is go ahead and enter a future where people share a love of living more in the mind and see a value in studying things that never sound required for survival on the surface, such as how Socrates talked with his philosophical pupils. I can only imagine the daily awe of learning while surrounded by marble columns featuring the sayings of Aristotle, Homer and others, New England fall foliage, and perhaps some flying buttresses. It sounds urgent, but it's only because the best time to leave is almost here. The present situation is I'm at the threshold of completing nine years at my rural school and crossing the real and symbolic road to enter the high school. I could easily turn toward town and the train station instead, where the map says the train lets out a very walkable sliver of distance from Harvard, unless a night arrival or books I may need to bring in the baggage make it wiser to flag a taxi for the campus dormitory or female rooming house, depending on what each would be asking.

Going on to the brief narration of my

background section, I need to let you know not to read mine and think this girl's trying to create a mood of shock and sympathy to gain a free ride or discount. The summary is that my mother became too sad and died when I was nine, and ordinary life got and stayed unusual for the two years it took to track down the steady foster situation I still enjoy here. Things in between include moving out of the house due to my father's problems and then his death due to a sudden head vein explosion the next year, living with an aunt who didn't have raising another girl in mind, living with my art teacher and then getting moved out of there because of judicial branch confusion, getting assigned to live with my grandmother who soon sickened, lingered, and died, loving school as well as close friends throughout, reading like a fiend, having to move out of another house on Christmas and walking up the road to the house of girls run by a foster lady, thus my name Ellen Foster.

If I had the job of selecting a well-rounded group of individuals to come to my college, I would worry about an underage orphan with a list of obstacles showing up and being a misfit, but I want to emphasize that I get along well both at school and at home. My foster mother is not pleased with my educational outlook and has tried to correct it on this end, but the private school here is the Academy of the New Dawn Apocalypse, and the school board said forced busing was enough upheaval so they cannot allow students to bend the rules to skip grades or change schools, unless a person needs Braille material or rails. When I asked her about Harvard, she said she'd seen college careers pan out for several piano and mathematical prodigies on public television, so nothing would be lost by me giving it a try with only offering more general skills of the mind. I realize that it could not be more expensive, which is why I need to emphasize that I know how to work and don't at all mind it.

On a typical morning at Harvard, for example, I could put in a few hours at the cafeteria, working the breakfast tray line, or at the gym, handing out baskets, although I have more experience in the library. I've been trained in all areas from ordering from the state depository to changing bulletin boards and worked in there alone for the three months of the librarian's knee surgery and malpractice case, and as she is now wheelchair bound and so much of a library involves reaching, I catch her up on a range of her daily duties. If you do not have the Dewey decimal system, I'd quickly adapt to your procedure. There's also the school store and canteen, and I've worked in the concession stand at high school sports games and during a series of wrestling extravaganzas in town and Billy Graham crusade shows.

Besides the current weekend jobs in home and church cleaning and magazine sales, I collect and write the school news, which runs each Saturday. It pays next to nothing, although everybody says the savings I can put toward Harvard from the cleaning, the food service, and magazines would pay for an ordinary education, if that's what I was after. I enclosed a copy of my column, Ellen's Tellin, to check on the possibility of getting on at the paper up there. One last idea is although I understand Harvard doesn't have a special education section, I wanted to let you know that I could substitute teach in the neighborhood for all types of unruly people based on my experience monitoring special students during their teacher's rest period.

Overall, it wouldn't be a problem for me to put in forty hours per week and also maintain top grades and participate in some extracurricular activities, such as intellectual clubs, debating leagues, and public speaking. I've been able to compete in speaking and would like to continue. Enclosed is the essay from the 1974 Woodmen of the World Youth Public Speaking contest which won in my state and then in Washington DC, entitled, Franklin Delano Roosevelt: King Arthur or Robin Hood? There was so much to send, I decided not to send the other one that won with the medical auxiliary entitled, Marie Curie: Madam and Mother, but I went ahead and enclosed The Cell Wall and the Surface of Hemingway's Stories: A Compare and Contrast, which won a scholarship to the humanities program Johns Hopkins in Baltimore puts on this October.

In closing, I hope everything helps show that I wouldn't be a fade-out or a person who turns to drink or dope when things become tough. I believe that anything is possible if you have the combination of love for what you're doing and the will to sit down and not get up until it's done. I realize the amount of work ahead and the costs, and even though the only scholarship plan I know about at this time is the one sponsored by the United Negro College Fund, which I am not eligible for with just the problem of being this young, I do have a mind, which we all agree is a terrible thing to waste.

Your friend,
Ellen Foster

One

ANYONE CONSIDERING MAKING an underage change in life, such as who you're going to live with, should know there's no way to avoid the government getting in on the decision, so try to be kind to the lady they'll send with a stack of tests and try to stay calm and do your best on them. I moved in here three years ago on Christmas Day of 1971, knowing as I knocked on the door that I was choosing this particular

replacement for life with my mother because the foster mother, Laura, had the
kind of home you'd be out of your mind
not to settle into for good.

My family was either dead or crazy, so
there wasn't the fall-back of concerned
loved ones. In fact, my mother's sister,
Nadine, who looks sane in public, had
created a no-room-at-the-inn situation
during her and her daughter Dora's fes-
tivities that caused me to strike out
walking for Laura's house.

The next summer Laura notified the
government that all was well and they
could go ahead and draw up her paren-
tal rights paperwork. Lo and behold a
letter arrived to say Social Service was
fine with our arrangement as long as I
could pass the mental stability tests
meant to prove whether I was too much
of a damaged goods personality to live
with a nice individual permanently or if
I needed to be demoted into a more
routine nightmare orphan home.

When Laura noticed me at the kitchen table with the letter and a resuscitated nail-biting habit, she said, You can't prepare for tests like these, Ellen, and when I called to say it's been nothing but a joy having you here, and I think I'd know by now if I needed to be sleeping with my eyes open because you were across the hall plotting waking nightmares, the woman said the tests were mandatory but they're a formality. There's nothing to worry about unless you chew your fingers so far down you can't write the answers.

She took me in for the tests the following Saturday morning, and just as I made the last multiple choice decision on whether I'd rather watch television or play baseball the lady told Laura and me to pardon the surprise but I needed to be shut up alone for another two hours with a kind of raw intelligence test they tacked on to the mental health portion. I said it was fine, just let me go to the bathroom and sharpen my pencil, not mentioning my suspicion that this was a fresh trick.

Laura took a breath and quietly blew her words out toward the lady, telling her in a way that could sound rude if you don't imagine it correctly, Well, she's here. She's willing and more than capable. I know the government's always created a certain amount of make-work, but it's worrisome for you to double tests that don't matter.

The lady said every time the court decided a child's life, the individual had to be run through particular tests before they could more or less turn you out into a new future. Pardon her again for not telling us about yet another final detail sooner, but a letter would be coming with instructions on when and where to take me for a thorough physical, courtesy of the government, down to the eyes, ears, and teeth.

She was smiling, hopeful we'd appreciate a free medical visit, but Laura blew gently again, saying, I'll take care of it. We have a family doctor. Shouldn't my fitness as a parent be a concern?

Laura wasn't being conceited, only picturing us in a line of teenage mothers with babies on their hips sucking root beer out of blue plastic milk bottles. Sorry to say it but I filled out that scene in the bathroom. When I got back and saw Laura running my pencils through a motorized sharpener, her tight method of movement and the way she dashed back her hair made her favor Ava Gardner, definite-edged in the midst of murky people, like in The Night of the Iguana when she's managing the old maid and the traveling women. The lady was fixated on Laura. She hadn't answered Laura yet, but she finally said, You can take her to the Mayo Clinic if you want to, and we know you're more than fit to take permanent custody of Ellen. How many pencils does she need?

More than she was led to believe, Laura told her, but since this is the last time, I'll let it be, and hope she'll be ready when I come for her. You know, it's Saturday.

She didn't say she was aggravated that the second test made us miss Willy Wonka and interrupted her plan to help catch me up on ordinary events by taking me to one childhood-type movie a month. She was aware of how when I was little, we stayed inside the house. The thought of heading out to the matinee movies or the family drive-in theater never arose due to different extremes. Now it was another thing available just to get up and go do. After American Bandstand, after the other two foster girls and I ate some sandwiches off the fold-out tables, we'd make the first afternoon showing and then walk around downtown, eating hot dogs and window shopping.

After the tests, Laura let me in the car, not all there, mumbling to me, And I'm even sorrier the downtown theater's switching over from Willy Wonka to Art

Garfunkel, of all people, in something you can't see and I don't want to. We need another theater. Who here would buy a ticket to watch Art Garfunkel with his clothes off?

I said, It's okay about missing the movie. They'll probably bring it back on the summer daytime schedule next year.

But you'll be too old for it then, she said. I'm aware you already are, but I thought it was important. How do you think you did on the tests?

I told her fine but draining, so I probably would've passed out in the theater. She said, Well, it's worked out for the best I suppose. We've got ten miles of straight road home if you want to rest your head in my lap.

I was sore from tensing in a hard chair for so long and didn't feel like touching right then, but I didn't want her to take it as I was upset about the movie and do the kind of out of her way thing she was prone to do and suggest we follow it to the next town. I was also guilty from being relieved I didn't have to sit through Willy Wonka and come out jangled up after two hours of watching overly eager singers and have to fix my face to say I'd just had a red-letter time of my life. Sweaty and sticky candy factory children hopping and singing around the chocolate vats, like they just happen to be living out the words to the songs, could irk you. I get more of a bang out of stories of realism that take place in the house or in the city, nothing on the open range, no forest or jungle except for Heart of Darkness, and except for Moby Dick, no man versus nature.

I was glad to feel her fingers on my hair though when I remembered the dark undersoul Willy Wonka had in the book and wondered if they'd allowed enough of him in the movie that you'd come out nervous about opening candy bars. People my age are old enough to know better, but I know some on my road, including myself, who're jubus about unwrapping a new cake of soap because of the nightmare possibility of seeing an innocent, trapped face staring up at you, permanently pressed there after a bad snatched hostage ordeal at Old Soap Molly's house. If you've lived a certain way and already have a lasting set of damages, you avoid what frightening fantasies you can.

It was only ten miles, but the weight of Laura's hand on my head and the tires underneath us knocked me out. I went straight to bed and just as I fell away, I was jerked back by the idea that the government was an expert at making you wait. I was facing another span of time I'd had to get to the other side of, not live wholly inside. After a month had passed, Laura called the Social Service lady, who said she couldn't help the backup, but remember the tests were only formalities. I wanted to shout and ask her if she'd ever needed permission to call her home a home or been jolted out of ease she'd trusted would come because the world couldn't possibly keep turning the wrong way. I pictured her arriving on the scene when I was too far past my ability to endure it and wreck what there was left of the life I'd reduced to reading with bleeding eyes and crawling to the supper table and crying on a pallet in the Easy Reader section of the library at school.

Laura would lean against the refrigerator, on the phone with my friends' mothers telling different versions of how tragic it was to watch me wait and what lengths she was tempted to go to if she didn't need to set a patient and legal example for me and the two other girls living with us, who started behaving like I was on their nerves for more than being odd now. Although Laura was evenhanded, they saw favoritism everywhere. There was nothing I could do except stay off to myself and do only the most basic portions of living the

grouped-together life while they slid farther and farther downhill from the high
state of niceness they seemed to enjoy
when I'd moved in.

Laura explained that it was part of
my nature to work off steam doing
things like chattering about the tests and
cleaning what wasn't dirty, and they
needed to respect what the basic notion
of being tested meant to me. She told
them, We all have a way we'd prefer
people to see us, and Ellen's very con-
scious of her abilities and nervous about
a judgment made about them the same
way I'd be uncomfortable if somebody
suddenly decided to measure my ability
to run a house, the same way you'd be if
you had to jump through hoops before
your families, well, something large like
that, could, well, be sorted out.

Laura left the room quickly, with
everybody understanding the three of
them weren't close enough for her to
open up the can of worms on the
wicked predicaments they'd been in. She

tended to them well and hoped it helped, knowing she couldn't mention their histories and fates without one of them defending the kind of person and behavior that deserved nothing. They stayed shut up together, blowing and sullen. I overheard them wondering if I'd have to leave if I failed, saying compared and contrasted to them I had it made with a dead family and an unknown future. Their mood improved when it dawned on one that at least they'd have the freedom to roam once they were out from under Laura's roof. You'd think they would've sympathized with my fears of getting dragged off to some gnashing-teeth type of place and suffering to sleep on a spotted mattress, hunched over, holding my tennis shoes and clean socks with the blue dingleballs from getting robbed off my feet by some bloodthirsty orphans.

Finally, the lady got here and got to the point pretty immediately, saying that figuring out what to do about me had taken more time than she'd expected because they'd graded the tests twice and then had to consider more complicated plans after my IQ popped up in the range where people are prone to losing their ration and nursing along gibberish plots to overthrow the government. Then she wanted to stress that my destiny could also simply be nonproductive.

Laura said, Okay then, we need to put this news, such as it is, toward making the rest of her life better than it's been. It sounds simple, but it isn't. You know what I mean? But this has to mean she can stay. Am I right?

Yes, the lady said, and what Ellen needs to realize her full potential involves nothing you can't handle, although I've had some troubling doubts about her school. The prisons are filled with people who dipped and dipped and then dallied out of boredom, so if she's dissatisfied with a particular class or drifting, she can study that subject

independently in the library, one or two
or all of them, whatever works best.

It was only Mrs. Delacroix in the library, and even though she'd gladly give
you her all, that didn't come out to too
much. She'd run the lunchroom until
she suffered mistakes during a leg vein
operation, so now she was bound to a
wheelchair and waiting for a lawyer to
make her doctor pay for destroying her
ambulation. She had a different way of
speaking she chalked up to Louisiana,
and although I loved listening to her,
you don't want somebody stewing their
language around taking a stab at training you for college. I explained some
concerns, such as the only book Mrs.
Delacroix had read was The Power of
Positive Thinking, and me being left to
wander around unorganized in so much
information and asked whether help was
coming from anywhere else. The lady
described more about the lesson plans
for self-guided people in my category

and said she'd explained all this to the principal. There'd also be bottomless advice available from the college education teachers who'd drawn up the guidelines.

Fighting not to see myself reclused in with Mrs. Delacroix, changing her leaking vein bandages and accumulating nervous isolation tics, I told her I got along with people very well and had been going around with the same group from my road since we started to school. I wasn't the kind who slopes around and eats lunch alone. You wouldn't see me, I told her, and say I look lonesome.

She swore this wouldn't cut me off from civilization, and I'd be able to do as much or as little as I wanted to do extracurricularly. Then looking at Laura, the lady said, Ellen's imagination's getting away with her, and that's part of what we've been mindful to keep satisfied.

Pardon me, Laura told her, but even if it was possible to keep someone with such a high curiosity entirely occupied, I don't think the goal of giving Ellen what she needs should be to keep her out of trouble, which she's shown no inclination to get into anyway.

She told Laura she agreed it was miraculous I'd stayed free of delinquencies, and then she handed me the stack of outline materials and the court papers which had been stamped to approve me permanently. Our first job is to see to the body and the mind, she said, and I think it's safe to say that between your new situation at school and this wonderful home, you should flourish, but I want to remind you that to whom much is given, much is expected.

I had to ask, Who expects it? How much is much?

Sighing so long and hard the wind almost knocked me down, she said, Ellen, you need to consider how fortunate you are. You need to thank your living God to be alive and well and blessed with the extraordinary good sense He gave you, and if you're ever called upon to endure again, I trust, after everything you've been through, you'll be the kind of young woman who will suffer gladly.

So, that was it, I told Laura. I never have to peel the back of my legs off government seating again.

To celebrate, she had an outsized, overly stuffed floral chair I'd tried out downtown delivered to the corner of my room, and for the next three years, if you were looking for me in the house, if I wasn't in the kitchen or Laura's room, I was in the Mamie Eisenhower chair, reading books from the library the handyman veteran installed in the living room after the college education office told Laura about ordering used books from the mail-order professor's catalog. There's a ladder leaned against the shelves, not on roller wheels on a gold bar, just the one the man left behind after Laura mistakenly paid him in full before he'd finished the final touches. We made it match by stripping off the paint drips and spills and staining it the New England home library deep tone of chocolate.

Two

THE SYSTEM WAS FINE FOR THE first two years. Then last year Holden Caulfield began eating worry into me about whether I wanted to go through with crossing the road to the regular rural high school, which would be for all intents and purposes my old school but with ashtrays outside the main hall. I knew I couldn't keep up with Holden and his crowd on matters such as clothing and leather luggage, but competing for grades didn't seem that difficult. I had the advantage of a history of working like a dog while they seemed to give themselves a great deal of time off for sports and touring dates around New York City.

I made sure to thank Laura for everything she'd done before I went into her bedroom one evening and sprung on her how I needed more. She had house and family magazines spread around, and when she shoved them over for me to sit down and tell her what I needed, I had to say that all I knew was I was feeling more and more squirmy about spending three years at a school with everybody whose ambitions were lowered down to just the rural style of life. Since the only choice of private education was the Apocalypse school, I didn't know what to do about this sensation that my future was being threatened into impossible.

She more than understood and said she'd call the Social Service lady the next morning, but for now, if I wanted a view into a world where too much of a good thing spelled more trouble than having nothing, I should crawl up with her and read an article on the swanky home life of Patty Hearst. You can't watch Citizen Kane accumulate his trove and not picture yourself ringing the doorbell at Xanadu and having him quiz you on your various interests and needs before he laughs heartily and says he's been waiting for someone like you and he'd be honored if you'd allow him to set you up in a fabulous dormer room and keep you in clothes his magazines advertise and then send you to college well-versed in conversation.

The government fell short of a situation Citizen Kane and the modern Hearst crowd could set you up in, but at least the lady came quickly this time. When Laura phoned her up, she'd alerted her to bring the next height of ideas, and so she splayed out what she'd investigated into across the kitchen

table, pointing to brochures on different
talent camps and weekend college semi-
nars, lining out what they could cover
on fees and transportation and what we
had to pay, using the tone you associate
with the man listing the prices of soy-
bean and pork belly futures on the news.
The figures could be shaking up Idaho,
but not to hear him tell it. The difference was the lady was talking about
sums that can alter your life, and I didn't
know whether her mind had come un-
connected from her mouth and words
like, well over a thousand, meant nothing to her, or, if she looked around at
our stuff and style and assumed we had
that kind of money casually lying
around in the black box with stars lac-
quered on to it, which actually did look
perfect for holding strong-smelling
stacks of new cash. Laura was also behaving like a pod person, taking in the
news with no expression, nodding some,
taking notes, I was scratching, chewing,
sucking, blowing, sweating, and puls-

ing, barely able to sputter out, I had no idea I was turning out to be this expensive. Do they have some variety of greenbacks stamp deal or a coupon book like the chamber of commerce has for holiday hotels and rent-a-cars? I'm sorry, but something has told me these IQ camps ran more in the thirty, forty dollar range.

Why, the lady asked, would you think that?

I said, money and the mind usually seem to live so far apart, and I'm sorry, but you expect Harvard to be priced this high, but not weekends with the chess crowd. I really thought you'd go off on what this one brochure's making sound like a brain isolation retreat and rough it more on the cheap, but it quotes you between six and eight hundred dollars to sleep in the sand dunes and fight fleas and get up at the crack of dawn to operate on fish.

This one, Laura said, in Baltimore, this humanities program sounds custom-made for you. It's next October at Johns Hopkins.

A wave of sick faintness I hadn't felt in a while washed through me. I'd wanted to be through with the kind of hot, crackling black coming down over my eyes like a shade shot through with pierces of light. I needed to droop to the floor before another wave came down or to get to the bathroom somehow to press my face against the tile and wait for the acids to stop churning up and melting the tender tissues inside my throat. Laura reached for my hands. There was security in knowing she recognized a mood coming on and wouldn't allow me to pass out and die from a sharp blow to the head on the way down, but I didn't want her to comment on how cold and clammy I was and have Social Service panic over my well-being.

I clamped my hands between my knees and spoke quietly to keep my stomach less disturbed, only partway hearing myself over questions screaming inside me, asking if I was ever going to heal from the plague of frustrations. Other people don't have to chew up good time recovering nor see their hearts throbbing through their undershirts because the person who committed to caring for them promised to do what it takes to give them something they need.

Laura, I said, it's okay, and thank you, but a weekend in Baltimore runs about what I thought college costs. It's too much. Actually, it's way too much.

Laura said, Well, this is a new world I'm in now, but you seem to get what you pay for there, so don't worry.

When the lady said educational money was easily had from civic groups that doted on ambitious youth, another wave of the blues washed through me. I could see Laura sitting on the sofa, shivering with blankets around her shoulders while her bathwater's boiling in a pot she's had to hang by the fireplace, going without to repay the debt I'd caused by spending like the wind at a high-IQ camp. I said, Mam, I think those are all ideas, but it isn't like we're part of the have-nots, and when you get down to the reality of it, taking a train or a plane for a weekend at a famous college isn't the kind of thing I have any business doing.

Laura said, Ellen, didn't you see these brochures?

I said, I did, and everything looks interesting, but I'll be fine with the way things are at school. This other's too different, it's too all-out. It's for people who do things like spending a thousand dollars on clothes, but I appreciate the thought. If we found a pearl in some oysters or won the Kentucky Derby, then I'd be more able to do it.

The lady had been sopping her cookies in her coffee and eating them all over her lips to where you regretted offering them to her, but she'd been doing that a while. Then, after I was through talking, she stopped and dotted her mouth with a napkin saying, Well, this is certainly a changed you I'm hearing. Three years ago, the little girl I tried to talk to was so hostile and defensive she wouldn't have given me air in a jug.

Laura said, I don't think it's necessary to make it sound like she was ruthless back then, though if it seemed that way, you can bet it was the best she could do. I didn't get her here, the government certainly didn't. Her attitude is why we're sitting here now. You know I know from ruthless children, you've certainly sent more than my quota to me.

The lady put her saucer at the edge of the table and shoved her crumbs over into it, keeping her head down, so she wouldn't move on toward the subject Laura had just come very close to, of how I'd had to strong-arm the other two girls back into the foster care system when they finally caused more chaos than Laura and I could stand earlier in the year. She left without mentioning it, saying on the way out the door only to remember her old advice about much being expected from those who were given as much as I'd been blessed with. Although she worded it differently, she ended by saying she trusted that two people as clever as Laura and me could figure out how to get me off this road if we believed I was so different I required special and high-tone surroundings to fulfill my destiny in.

While I was putting the program brochures away in the rolltop desk Laura kept household paperwork in, I opened my savings passbook and told her what I had thus far wouldn't cover cake decorating classes at the night college over by the lumber mill. Then I closed the top and lay on the sofa and gazed at cartoons, waiting for my stomach to cool down. She pulled a blanket over my legs and began going through the house and rambling for things that needed to be washed or hit with the iron a second time. She finished sooner than usual, and there she stood by my feet, screeching the ironing board open and plugging in the iron and holding her hands around it while it warmed, favoring Ava Gardner again when she's holding on to the handlebar of the rolling cocktail-hour cart and converting it into a steadying symbolic rock.

Laura always called for me to come spit on the iron because she knew I liked hearing it sizzle, but when she offered, my stomach didn't feel right enough to be up. When I told her I needed to lie there and feel like dirt a few more minutes, she said, I know you do.

I said, I don't want to be smart-mouthed, but you know I didn't come here with a dowry. I brought one hundred and sixty-six dollars in a paper sack, and that's earned about a dollar in interest since then. If I were you I'd be relieved if somebody said they were willing to stay home for free.

I believe you'll get a scholarship, she said, but if you didn't or if it isn't enough, we'll figure something out. Any number of things can be done, so at the very least, I want you to plan on going to this program.

I said, And when you fall into deep debt to pay for my college and I fall in front of a bus and can't work to repay you so you can repay the bank, ask me if I hadn't seen it coming every time the collector drove off with my father's late-payment merchandise. We have some interesting stories already going on here, and I don't see any plots that involve you living in more or less a drainage tube in Calcutta because of me. You know I have to go by the theme of working to get the money you need for something. It's a simple if-then, Laura. If you did that, you can do this. I don't see how it varies from you always getting up and doing the nastiest job of the day first.

Moving my legs aside to sit down, she said, Getting the best education possible isn't like bleaching grout. And listen when I tell you, a girl your age has no business thinking about death and taxes. Repaying me for this course or the others or college or anything, Ellen, shouldn't occur to you. I'd expect some gratitude, being human I suppose, but that's the extent of it, so if it doesn't concern me, there's no reason for it to grind you this way.

The only problem is you don't realize how dangerous it could be to take what you offer. They said I wasn't damaged, but this is damage, this is a mess I've brought to your house, only you don't consider it the selfish way I would if I were you. I can fix this. You'll stay glad I'm here, but not if I take what's yours. I know how to get what I need done. It's real and true and simpler like this.

She rubbed a circle on my leg and patted the place down before she hopped up and unplugged the iron. Looking at the television, she said, I didn't know they were running Dark Shadows again. I've seen you watch that, so just rest with it and I'll come iron later.

Laura asked for nothing but the honor of having a girl like me, to look after and hold her daily conversations and customs with. When I considered the harm I could do Laura, it was embarrassing, revolting, and much more horrible than the idea of her paying for my education. There was the force to feel the wind off of, the sting of a slap from a person too turned in on herself to rehearse how the wounds would feel and too familiar with them to stop and measure their speed and imagine the surprise someone like Laura must feel each time she closed herself in her room to adjust herself to it, sparing me from watching her recover.

Life closed twice when my mother and father died, worlds apart but gone, and now I wasn't certain I could outlast a third event, of Laura leaving, even in the house with me but not present, always turned in, protecting herself from me.

Even if I could trick myself into counting on a miraculous machine of the gods swooping in at the last minute, I realized how risky it'd be to count on something like a wealthy benefactor to hear about my plight and sympathize when I didn't have a sports skill to get my name around or hail from an inner city successful people like to donate to in memory of their roots. You can also be musical and get supported, but the farthest I'd gotten toward developing my talent was thinking about taking piano lessons from the preacher's wife, so I wasn't involved in anything that'd make somebody like Stevie Wonder or Sammy Davis Jr. take notice.

Then I'd think, How would they even hear about you on your road? Talent scouts don't tend to blow through here. There wasn't an uncle in the television industry who could get Walter

Cronkite to inspire all his viewers to donate a dime to help pave the rest of the
road to the future.

A couple of weeks later, on the morning this present school year started, I
was standing on the edge of the road,
looking back at the square hedge bushes
and the clean brick steps Laura and I
had sat on after supper so often that
summer, still seeing the vision I'd created of the dump truck sent with best
regards by the gang at CBS World
News, to pour a silver stream of dimes
into a massive mound in the yard.

The bus arrived and the doors
opened and I got on and said hey to
people I felt like I hadn't seen in a year
although I just saw them yesterday at
the store or downtown Saturday buying
new clothes. As we lost sight of my
house, I knew Laura was about to take
her bath and listen to the morning
shows through the open bathroom door.
She could relax well with nothing to re-
sent. I couldn't put her out by leaving

her. Whatever I did about leaving, I'd have to accomplish through realism, and beyond Laura and the people on the bus I loved, I didn't trust much. More than anything, I trusted myself to work and knew what I felt about the kind of individuals who mash the snooze button on the clock and stay there, continuing to roll and wallow.

Once I began taking on jobs and studying like a fiend, I got a sideline benefit. Working constantly up to the utmost possible edge of sleeping kept the space my mother had left more filled. If leisure wasn't well-planned, worry over where she was now would move into the time like a bumptious stranger and addle me out of a place in line. That sliver between wakefulness and sleeping was particularly hazardous if I left what happened inside it to chance. All hell could break loose, and I loathed feeling forced to search for my mother in the flames and listen for her in the screaming of everyone her funeral

preacher had said was confined to torment by an outraged God who didn't
need or want help carrying out His will.
Sometimes, I used the time to think of
ways she could've been spared. Random
as science was, there was more justice in
the laws of nature, more mercy, well-
deserved, than in rules that said her decision to die was unforgivable. Whoever
could claim that she had enough gall to
throw God's gift back in His face didn't
know her very well, but unless she'd
been allowed to get in on the tickets
they give to people like pygmies and
life-long coma victims who have never
been exposed to religion. If I believed
the rules, I had to believe they applied
to her, so I took a personal doubt holiday that will last until undeserved cru-
elty, then, now, and thereafter, seems
acceptable.

The only road to silent peace was
through the words I wrote down to
keep, more for the sounds than the
meanings, that were always able to carry

me to where I was able to rest, holding
back the old sounds and scenes that have
had time to organize themselves inside
me and grow as strong as men, so you
learn by heart and you're grateful to say,

Philanthropist, opulent, honorific,
  keening,
Tumult, tumultuous, compatible,
  breast-feeding,
Cinema, efficient, evermore, cellar
  door,
For I have eaten ashes like bread and
  mingled my drink with weeping,
That I may learn in my own life and
  away from home and friends
What the heart is and what it feels.
Beadsman, celibate, cenobite, friar,
Mendicant, palmer, pilgrim, prior.
Mother of God, Amen, Mother of
  God, so be it.

Three

LOOK AROUND MY HOUSE AND SEE why the beauty here knocks me off my feet every few minutes of the day. There's a kind of love behind the thoughtfulness you see when you open the door to a room that draws you inside to sit down and gaze, enjoying how welcomed you feel and trusted as well not to spoil things. How many times have you been in a place where the lady of the house is so wadded up by fear of spilling on the sofa she's kept it enclosed in plastic, and how many people have you visited who lacked the edge of sophistication to realize that they were supposed to unwrap the lampshades once they got them back to their living rooms from the display living rooms at Sears? You see Laura's confident tastes and her refusal to let life revolve around terror of stains impressing visitors when they come in, and even though other women on our road may not be able to go through with finally stripping their plastic when they leave here, they behave like it's the amazement it is that she can interior decorate like out of a magazine and mix tones of paint in brave and unique ways without anything about herself or her house making them feel like lesser housekeepers or victims of families that wouldn't appreciate anything new they might try.

Martha's mother visits when the store is closed of a Sunday afternoon and takes a nap in the guest room, generally without letting her family know where she is. If you saw the wreckage from Martha's five brothers in the house, you'd know why she parks where you can't see her car driving by and refuges in what she calls the peace of mind room down here. Before I saw it clearly, Laura explained her resting as she was making her a pot of tea to wake up with, saying, Women hide women, Ellen. Sometimes you have to make one wash her hair and go downtown, and sometimes you have to help one have a little rest and rustication from her life. And don't tell Martha her mother's here when she's missing. It's only two or three hours, but the child will decide she's poisoned and want to nag her mother for the antidote.

I said, But if Martha or her brothers have an accident or something, and they can't find their mother, what about an emergency like that?

You see it, she said, through your eyes, but the reality is there's another able adult in the house, asleep in front of a football game, and that's the only time he's in the house all week, so he can learn to be on his feet and alert if his children need him.

I didn't need to ask Laura whether she needed to be hidden from me. I followed her down the hall with the tin of mail order shortbread she allowances out for visitors.

You open the door to the guest bedroom that used to be the scrambled, moxed mess the other two foster girls lived in and see the fabric coordinated, not matching but still good, on the padded window seat, the bed, and the straight, long-hanging curtains. Stay here a while and learn that a suit of clothes drapes on your body, drape is a verb, not a noun, and you wash your hands in the sink, not the zinc, which is not to say my way of speaking was oafish before I got here. My mother's history had her say, like Laura, stockings instead of hose, undergarments for bloomers, drawers, panty leggings, and step-ins, and if we'd had more than a few belongings in our house, they would've been arranged in this appropriate way, like a cottage motel royalty would say they found agreeable to stay in. I had to move a silver rose bowl, for example, to put the tea tray down, and when I set it on the dresser, I had to move aside a dozen or so kooky windup tin toys we keep there for Starletta to stay occupied with when she comes over.

Taking a look around the living room, there's a wooden bowl of many woods on the mantel and two pewter candlesticks at each end, and hanging over it is an old window we made into a picture frame, and where the window-lights should be are scenes of us on various holidays and one of Starletta and me dressed out as macaroni and cheese on the first Halloween I was here. On the round cherry table nearby is a tall lamp and a slender, floral painted shade and a golden frame with a picture of me fishing Starletta out of the bobbing for apples barrel that same year. Laura's theory is you keep the public surfaces free of everything except for a lamp, a book, and a thing, so the end tables by the sofa have a lamp, a box we keep arrowheads in, and books you think are important for people to pick up and leisurely read in: We Are Your Sons, about Julius and Ethel Rosenberg and how their sons fiercely believe they weren't criminals, a biography of Franklin and Eleanor Roosevelt, and a book of T. S. Eliot poems called Four Quartets, which helped when some Jehovah's Witnesses dropped by and didn't want to understand that a poet could work religion into his themes.

One thing to note is watch out when you sit on the large leather ottoman over near the kitchen. If the hidden wheels aren't braced, it'll slide out from under you, or if you hold on and push against the sofa, you can jump the threshold

and ride past the appliances and the
sink, usually ending up in the area in
front of the back door, where you clean
dirt off your feet. It's not a room specif-
ically though it goes by the name mud-
room. I haven't ridden the stool since I
moved in, but since we changed out the
kitchen linoleum for hard tile, there isn't
a problem with pushing Starletta. Laura
dreads Stuart wanting to take off on it,
banging dents, but it has to do with
his size and how he doesn't realize the
force of his own weight, so as long as
you're not that heavy and know to do it
once and then stop, she'd say go ahead.
All she asks is you not behave like you
were raised in a floored pen, which isn't
a problem for people who quickly pick
up on the news that things are a rung
or two above the typical, tear-it-up
wrestling den. There's no wooden fork
and spoon on the wall, no easy recliner,
the pale yellow quilted satin she sewed
lays across the arm of the sofa, not
across the back, like in an invalid house,

nothing sateen or shag, no burnt orange or vanilla incense, no sign saying to Bless This Mess and no mess.

Laura despises filth and chaos and believes there's self-respect in getting up and doing what calls for bleaching first, and since the other two girls left, she hasn't had to endure anybody struggling against the order here, which is not to name me perfection, but glancing slights like faking sleep when I don't want to delve into the day or shifting when she reaches to touch me because of something like a bad monthly mood that takes things beyond your ability to be caressing are nothing in comparison to how the other girls treated her. If you don't want to sleep for a few days, go into her room after she's slowly closed herself up in there to sit on the edge of her bed a few minutes and recover from some ugly choice you made to be stubborn. Apologize and hear it's fine or she needs time because of a remark you made about how you'd put out a leg and thumb to Baltimore before you'd accept a charity dime for the train fare, and then go back and ball yourself up in the nice chair she bought you and regard the words that come out of your mouth and cringe at what a big shot you sounded like. Make a mistake with your mouth in this beautiful place with the woman who rescued you from the fate of strangers and uncaring aunts, and see how much power you have and how dangerous and easy it is to slip into being the kind of girl who damages women. Then total how far a distance there is between you right then and women who love enough to keep a friend hidden of a Sunday afternoon and waken them with English tea in a china pot and a tin of biscuit treats they can't have at home because everything gets consumed out from under them.

You hope it's only human nature that makes you uncivilized around the edges sometimes, and you tell yourself you aren't like the others who took too much. Compare and contrast the freedom you feel to breathe freely and go in and out of the rooms without worrying about opening a door to their rough company on the other side. In the girls' bedroom I would hear males being big shots, talking about their deals like somebody sixteen has business enterprises, ripping into the Little Debbie cakes I took for lunch and leaving the box gaped empty in the pantry, flagrant about behaving like they owned the place when Laura wasn't here and crawling in the windows when she was. She eventually found them out by following a trail of sorriness, and one evening when she came in from the movies early and cleaned her way to them, stooped over with their floor trash in her hands and opened the door on their party, the clash and conflict I'd expected didn't happen.

She said, If you don't live here, get

out, and you two, sit here until I can speak. I'm going to think. Then I'll speak.

I heard her on the phone to Starletta's mother, saying the girls were growing up downhill and she was afraid, she said, on account of the quality and quantity of attention they were after. I thought she'd say I was a relief or my problems were at least not proning me toward sexuality diseases, but she didn't, and although the girls tried to move the topic off them and onto things like how un-healthy it was for me to read all night and how I existed to turn them in for minor trivialities, she wouldn't be varied off them. She taped rules on the refrig-erator, which I thought gave out too much world to operate in, especially for the busty one with the new driving li-cense, but they only felt more fenced in. They tore beyond the outline and pressed in all directions while I watched what I'd come here for become com-pletely disdone.

The minute Laura cranked the car to be gone more than an hour, they were phoning up characters to come over, common, hostile old friends and relations in the main from their old lives, untrustworthy people. They sniffed around Laura's bedroom belongings and stole her sample bottle of Chanel Number 5, leaving her to think it'd fallen off her dressing table into the trash I'd then carried out and disposed of. I had to stand between two strumpets and a woman disappointed over her only perfume, wondering if family loyalty to girls with evil gene pools and hordes of imprisoned people in their genealogy meant keeping the truth in until my lips exploded. You wondered if she'd say I shouldn't have told her because family members have permission to be treacherous and protect one another, but I wasn't aware of that because instructions on everyday life in the family unit weren't installed in me young.

I hit the limit of the rock and the

hard place on a school vacation day when Laura drove Starletta's mother and her to the teaching hospital to meet a new doctor. When she said she'd be gone from dawn to dusk, you could see the wheels turning with the girls' plans on the good time that was due to be had by all. They kept enticing me to visit people, but I said I'd rather stay in my room, which they took as a sign I'd be lurking and phoned people up saying Old Ellen might find herself on the far side of a locked door and so on. Laura hated to trust them, but they said they recognized she had the one nerve left, and if they danced on it, that would be that. Earlier than they usually managed to wake up for school, they were sneaking their favorite gang of foulmouth grabbers in, including a boy who bragged he was AWOL and several who looked like they'd be diseased down there. Then I heard the clothes dryer buzzer go off over the record player and racket, and when I opened the laundry room, I knocked into the army criminal and a girl with face skin that looked like potato chips participating in something so far toward sex you could call it sex.

They created scenes of chaos they couldn't put back in order fast enough. When Laura came home early and walked into this one, she went to her bed and cried, mainly, she said, because she hadn't left them in the middle of the night, this had been a weekday morning, which made her feel like something not quite violent but definitely unfriendly had jumped out at her, stubborn deaf and blind to the day she'd spent doing a good thing. The hours bundled into stacks of days she'd spent on them that were now looking like futile time she could've used elsewhere. When they all finally left, including the girls, I said, If I was you, I'd call the veteran and have him change the locks and stand in here and turn some tough love on them when they set up banging to get in.

She said, I know, and it's sad, this route they've taken, but the families they come from are sadder, and it's only a couple of months until things at home are straight enough for them to be back there. So maybe let's try to be patient. Maybe you could stay overnight at a friend's if things aren't comfortable here.

I said, I don't mean to say it's turned upside down, but I don't know if the one behaving ought to be the one put out. This wasn't part of the program when I said I wanted to be here permanently.

Not put out, she said, just a couple of nights, if they do something like this again.

I said, But why can't they just be decent instead of me having to pack another suitcase? Part of what I was given was a fair amount of patience, but those girls expect to keep draining the well continuously. My family may not be in jail, but they're still either dead or crazy, and I'm the one here losing sleep over taking a sliver of pie.

You can't make people behave, she said, by force of will, and you should try harder not to panic when things feel a little out of place.

I said, It's the middle of the day and somebody's crying in the house. What if one of them gets a baby in here? Suppose they drag people in that hurt us, not our perfume, but us bodily? And they're not upset right now. They're at Wright's Chick Shack, laughing about us in the parking lot. It seems to be very relaxing not to have anything expected of you, but I'm worn out watching it. I thought it'd be peace for more than a few minutes.

Yes, she said, I know you did, and when I can think about what to do about them, I'll do it, but you may just have to be patient. There aren't many people who'll take older girls, even briefly.

Because we cause so much commotion, I told her. That's what people think.

She said, You know you don't.

I said, No, it's okay. Then I left the house and rode my bicycle down to Martha's store and used the pay phone to call the foster office and say I was sorry to report it, but I knew of some girls the foster office needed to come on back out here and load up because through no fault of their new mother's and the hoopla they'd created on their own, they were bordering on being out of hand, and if anyone needed evidence, they could be found drinking alcohol out of sacks outside a take-your-clothes-off place in town, where one or the both of them was nursing an ambition to work. When the lady asked where Laura was all this time, I said, Same place as she always is, at home and hearth, doing the very best she can.

Laura was supposed to be told only so much of what I'd said, but riding back home, as my forearms began to numb and hot stomach acids began to attack, I realized you can't trust the government after Watergate. Riding to my house felt so much like riding to my doom that I sat on the steps when I got there, hoping she'd be worried enough around dark to speak to me in relief rather than with a sting in her voice. If I hadn't been worried about being seen by somebody riding by, one plan was to turn the bicycle over in the ditch and have it lay there on top of my body a while, anything not to hear her say I'd destroyed two girls to save myself, and I'd never be the kind of woman who shelters a friend if I was this conniving about putting them back in their pasts before people there were wholly healed and ready for them.

The crunch of the granite rocks in the driveway is generally loud, particularly if the bicycle tires need air in them, but when I rode up, it sounded like I was grinding them between my ears. I knew she heard me because the front curtains parted, and when the door opened, I exploded into a wild kind of weeping just as she said, Well, just sit here and get pulled together because you want to be in fairly good shape when they show up for this emergency investigation, or they may take you, too, take you, take me, take them, close the house down, Ellen, and take us all. You see, you said the girls were out of control, so it naturally follows that I'm allowing them to run wild and leave the windows cracked for the boys and get by with all these other offenses you must've done an excellent job listing.

Mother of God, I said, they're after you? Are they taking me?

Ten or fifteen years from now, she said, I'm sure it'll be hilarious, but right now it's not. You described this as a mess of an ordinary day.

I said, I was trying to fix it.

Patience, you needed to manage for another few weeks. I told you.

But, I told her, it sounds like a long time. It's been so little of life, you know what I mean to say, right, and now they'll end it again?

She pushed the ottoman over and sat down with her knees jabbed up to mine and told me, Your life, your life isn't the only one here.

But I was making something of it, I told her. They were just treating their life like a motel, you know, not attached, and I've been making things.

Yes, she said, you have, and they've been alive and doing fairly what they've known how to do at the time.

Martha's oldest brother had told me about seeing them in unsightly places in town, and I had a sudden picture of them going through a siren arrest and having my name on their lips while their mug shots were taken. I said, Maybe they weren't that bad. I guess I can take it. Let me call the foster office and say I lost my head and passed some false rumors or something and you were upset over something else I didn't know about yet.

So instead of us sounding like two extremely mean-spirited and disturbed people, we'll sound like Lucy and Ethel, she told me. If I were you, I'd dry my face and get back to whatever I was doing, and don't phone up anybody else, either here or behind the meat counter down at Martha's place. Let me get dinner together and let me manage this, and Ellen, think before you do this the next time, think a thing completely through.

I did, I said.

When? On your way down there?

I said, I've thought about what to do once I started living all my life, and I thought this was how you did it. I don't need supper though. Martha made ham sandwiches while I was on the telephone.

When I got to my room, I couldn't rest, so I wrote some on how things had corroded so darkly from where the girls had been the first day I saw them with Laura with a kind of bright light of bliss around them and thought they were set to live out the orphan American dream. I stayed out of my skin, thinking about how to be a part of this group that seemed to take for obvious granted that you change your underwear daily and hand-wash your brassiere in Ivory Snow once a week, and when the moment came for me to find a place to live again, even though there's only the one road everything in my life has always oper-ated off of, all the roads led to here.

The roads would come together here and conclude. I'd move elsewhere for college eventually and do the epidemic disease research and come home for hol-idays bringing Laura unique presents from across the international date line. If she wanted to, she could come with me a few times, the way Starletta's prob-ably going to do. This was the story I'd started writing here, and when it was snatched by people who interrupted with jangling, ill-fitting contributions, I couldn't throw up my hands and let the work and words scatter like October leaves on me. If you want a rhythm in your life as dependable as the seasons, you can allow only so much outlandish weather in before things become too confused to repair.

I was finishing the picture of me staggering up out of the ditch, miraculously clean when Laura came in, saying summarized, Don't trust that anything you mox in again like this is going to work out according to your specifications, and believe me, your life is going to be enough to keep up with from now on.

What happened was I landed on my feet because the girls were more or less off theirs by the time the lady got someone downtown to find them. Laura helped place them with married gym teachers she knew who had a knack for converting the wild, and by the time their families were ready for them, I heard they were routine girls who merely lived in town and reported to school and their part-time jobs on time.

I told Laura, It sounds like the girls probably slowed down out of a lack of somebody to get a charge out of and simple boredom.

Good, she said. There's a great deal to be said for boredom, not all of it bad. It leads to naps, although I know it'll be a while before I find you asleep during the day without sitting down to feel you for fever. It's you here now and the company we have wishes you well, so there's nothing stopping you from saying there's nothing to do so you're going to take your shoes off and get on top of the covers with your clothes on. You've learned to love and work well enough without a guidebook, and since I'm supposed to have one for you, I can tell you the next chapter's on rest though if you need a higher authority, I understand that citizens of Spain and France and I don't know where else are expected to rest, more than a little siesta. The idea of rest equals the idea of work, and I think they smear love throughout automatically, and I see another automatic thing, odd but nice, I think. Other people notice it to me, but I'm just hearing it. I sound like you, I hear old Ellen in me. Do you hear it? Listen to us, amazing.

Four

WATCH ME WALK, I CARRY MY hands to the sides. I don't lurch or slope. There's not a hunchback dome on my back. I can walk rested in the shoulders and loose armed, or I can walk with dignity, like a queen. After three years here, it's only loose ends left to manage, but when the list of things you have left to do on yourself includes items such as healing from terror that comes and goes and frequently gets in your way, it looks like the large job of work it still is. The good news was I was on the brink of October.

If you think about October's role in the calendar, you'll see it was custom-created to relieve the sensation of unsettledness and the mingling fears and needs that still edged in if I took a brief vacation, and let my mentalities go lax the way people my age who don't have to feel old as vampires have the privilege to do. October promises a difference and brings it, the changes it says are coming always come. When the air crispens, it splurges on symbols, dropping beautiful proof at your feet. It doesn't lie or leave out, saying death will be around eventually but only because life was already here, and here's some color and snappy weather and flocks of birds flying south to allow you to breathe deeply in trust that the universe knows what to do and when to do it. There won't be haywire shocks to wound the sky and shatter down another dose of jagged edges. October knows you've had enough.

The rhythm of the world out here picks up when the farmer across the road begins plowing after he's brought in his main crops and sold them so he can settle his affairs at Martha's family's store and with the man who delivers his fuel oil. On he'll go around to businesses until everybody who helped him during the past year has been paid. Crossing the wide ditch and walking behind him as the ground's being turned over to expose arrowheads, which you may find one or several of, I was getting dirty in the good clothes I shouldn't have been over there in. When he gave me a couple of flints he'd found earlier, he didn't notice it to me or say he'd heard I wanted to go to college early, and I knew he had, he's Stuart's uncle. He talked about what he talks about, asking how one of his elderly ex-teachers is faring and whether I'm still passing my hard lessons in school.

After he's plowed the last row, he plants pumpkins to replace needed nutrients harsher crops like to strip up, and they grow so hurriedly that you look out the window again and he's over there, laying by. Look again and he's walking around, admiring them. By the middle of October, you can tell he's settled his bills not just by his improved posture but by how he's changed the sweat-banded cap he wore all summer to a Frank Sinatra hat he got out shopping with his family last Saturday. He's in a good mood because anybody is who's just been to Sears. I knew Stuart had also been there the second I walked down the aisle of the bus and tripped across his new Wolverines.

The people I go around with have never been model students, but October uplifts the least likely to read on his own and those with the worst collections of checkered report cards. Instead of getting to school and closing everything up in their lockers to droop around the rest of the day empty-handed, you'll see them thinking about the right books to take out. Stuart doesn't usually carry anything in his hands besides leftovers from our table's lunches and a black film between his fingers, but every October he comes in with a box of decorative gourds he brings for his teachers to think back on when they grade him.

He trogged past my locker, where some people were standing around with Starletta demonstrating the lit-up seasonal pin her mother varies on her dress collar. He stopped and said, Huh, a pumpkin? I thought it would've been a scarecrow pin. Huh, I aint studying pumpkins. Aren't they squash?

Luther said, I don't know, does it matter?

He turned back to Starletta, who's twelve now, with the body of a six-year-old and the mind of a friendly older toddler. Although she goes around oblivious, she's stuck beside me through thick and thin. Everybody knows her and loves having her around. She's the kind of famous person that if you don't know her, you know of her, and information like how she follows behind Luther a great deal and wears the changing seasonal light-up pins on her collar, though to me she's most known for her joy and gorgeous soul.

You want Luther to look like Marlon Brando but he doesn't. He lives on the other side of the pasture and has a semi-domesticated bobcat in his front yard. Setting the box down and wiping all over and around on top of his head with his arm, Stuart said, Only thing I know is I aint studying these vegetables. Swear before God my feet hurt, blisters, it's the Wolves. Mama said to treat them with lard, but huh, I guess I didn't.

Then you'll have to hobble, I told him, come on.

He knew I meant it was time for us to go out and sit on the low rock wall in front of the school. You could spend homeroom there if your class was on that side of the building and the teacher was willing to yell the roll out the window. Then everybody goes to their rooms and I'd recluse with Mrs. Delacroix and the books Johns Hopkins told me to have read in two weeks, which Stuart saw while we were on the wall outside. While he was repeating himself on what I was doing with a stack of new, thick books, where I was going and why, how I was getting there, when I'd be back, Marvin, Luther's first cousin, spoke over him to ask if I'd look over some poems he'd been assigned to compose. Then he got up to show them to me. Stuart didn't stop talking, he stared off and went on with the questions. With Starletta beside him, fixated on pulling the stem over and over to light up her pin, they made a world of a pair.

When Marvin brought me his opened notebook all the pages that should've had writing on them had it, there were no blank pages after doodles of guns and cars covering the first few.

That had to be October's enthusiasm.
Martha walked up late while I was trying to understand what his assignment
had been. She'd had to open the store,
so we all said, Huh, with Stuart and
went back to what we were doing, except for Luther who jumped up and
straddled the ditch for her to adore him
doing.

Stop or fall in, Martha told him. Boy
howdy, Luther, I'm a big fan of you
stretched across a drainage ditch. Heave
Stuart up and throw him. Throw his
box of squash. They're heavy, that'd be
sexy to me, wouldn't it, wouldn't it, huh,
huh. Thawing the fish locker this morning was a better use of my time.

He straddled and she hounded him
while Marvin kept on, She could of said
do rhyming, or not, I forgot to copy the
board down. I wisht I'd get a A on it
though, got a F now, didn't turn in
much when school started. Mumber
how hot it was? Me and deddy like to of

had to sleep in the chimley. Know how cool brick is?

He lives with his father in a very tiny house built close to the river, not like the holiday homes with the overhanging deck, but as in erosion. Laura trades turns with women who take them casserole dishes, and it's getting so steadily worse that by Christmas, water will flow through the door when they open it, given the sharp angled dip. I was in the library when the Earth Science class covered erosion and used his house as a kind of object lesson since everybody in there had either been to it or heard about it. He and his father probably had enough sturdy wood left for a lean-to, but he never mentioned an upcoming move or condemnation notice, and his school supplies were in excellent shape, so maybe if he had a dry place to study and sleep in, he felt fine. But I wasn't sure he would've seemed shaken if his house had took off drifting because of the way his basic nature and a life of hunting their non-casserole meals made his movements slowly careful.

I moved from wondering how he'd kept his homework clean to what he wanted me to fix. He said, I bet I'll get a A if you rhymed it, give you a dollar to do it.

The poem he'd written seemed meant to be shouted, and I'd need to turn the volume down on it first, but when I said for him to keep the dollar he was taking out of his pocket, Martha said, You phone me up, whining about the load these extra schools could put on Laura and how much Harvard costs, then turn a dollar down. Come get on at the store and have my mother tell you being lucky there's a store to work in is wages enough. You probably need, what, nine hundred thousand more of them? I wouldn't turn my nose up at one.

So I took the dollar, but for reasons I couldn't fathom, Luther took a B-plus on,

The First Day of Hunting Season

On the first day of hunting season,
You don't need another reason,
To rise early like the same bird,
You'll shoot from the sky, take my
    word.

The woods aren't dark and deep,
There's undergrowth and scrub by
    your feet,
But hunting's still the fall
    experience,
That keeps you feeling delirious.

Even in the winter gloom,
When you don't want to leave your
    room,
You have meat in the locker and
    maybe a pelt,
To help you remember how hunting
    season felt.

While he copied the poem in his
writing, Stuart said, I wish you wouldn't
talk to people when I want to say some-

thing to you, huh. I dislike them breaking in.

Nerves had beaded sweat on his head,
which he soaked up by pressing both
jacket sleeves in over his ears. I said, Are
you going to do your head or tell me
what the matter is?

Nothing, he said, I just dislike it is
all, but, huh, you still didn't tell me why
you brought all these books that don't
belong with you. I wish you'd say something on it before school takes in.

What hair he had was a light orange-
tinged yellow, but despite the sweat, he
wasn't carrying the odor you'd expect because of how October also brought personal hygiene benefits, coming between
the Indian summer heat and the winter
plague of cloakroom lice. Knowing
words, sweat, and tears would start
pouring, I didn't want to tell him about
Baltimore, but he could also make a day
long, so I told it rapidly and left to take
Starletta to her room when the first
names were yelled out for the roll. I'd be

under the compulsion to go to his house after school, where he'd be sitting on a bucket and poking a long stick at his family's continually burning rubber pile.

He sounds broke but you'd be surprised at how many times you'll be with his family and see them take out twenty-dollar bills to pay for things. It's very profitable for his father to drive up and down the interstate highways, relieving truck stops and service stations of shot tires he brings home and adds to the rubber pile, which is almost taller than the house, continuously smoking but not flaming. You'd think a man who does that would be putting his family in the strait of siphoning gas from the lawn mower to the car or taking twenty-three coupons to Martha's store to exchange for a penny and starting a fight over exactly what the fine print says the cash value is, things the family out here that eats off records does when nobody's needing any of the secondhand merchandise the father sets around in their yard. The first time I heard Laura use a vocabulary word was when she used lucrative, as in, I had no idea that trading in used rubber could be lucrative enough to keep Stuart's mother in Cadillacs. I'm stunned.

Since I've lived closer to this end of the road and nearer to Stuart than I did when we were little, I'm on a bucket beside him by the rubber pile fairly often. I wouldn't want it to sound like it's exploded more than once, and then only because of the gasoline and matches he threw on it last summer to protest his father leaving him there to nurse his mother through the insanity and hard recovery she suffered after her hysterectomy. Except for then, I haven't seen it flame, so I don't waste time picturing Salem executions there. You couldn't call it a pyre, but it's technically interesting because of the absence of odor, like Stuart's sweat, nobody smells it.

We could've adapted, but you wouldn't know unless you flagged down some strangers and asked them to stick their head out the window in the vicinity of Stuart's house and say whether they smell toxic fumes or smoke and supper rising from Starletta's house. That's mainly all we smell out here since Starletta's father died and her mama started soaking up the spare hours by volunteer cooking for the shut-in delivery program at some churches I helped her clean to raise educational money. The theory is the stranger would say, Smoke and supper, and go on. Stuart's mother is at ground zero and didn't birth maldeformed children. Even if we were to learn enough about toxic waste to believe different, I couldn't call the government and say I was reporting my neighbors for burning a dangerous hole in the sky.

Maybe I'd procrastinated on living in October the way I wanted to because it was hard to believe there could be pleasure in anything I hadn't earned. Maybe rotating around from a temporary state of the blues to the magic of all being well and perfectly fine became too much of a sure custom, like Starletta's pins. The prizes for talent and striving and the adaptation skills I'd used to get them would feel thrilling for a while, and work and words would keep my mother's empty space filled, but then everything would open again, more infinite ended, and I'd wonder if other individuals were rolling into the future this way and what they did to correct it.

I stayed at it, filling and carrying on a constant discussion with myself about how to live in a place that seemed endless and bottomless, studying nonchalant people who manage to cross streets, open doors, drink from water fountains, or tie their shoes without needing to scream about how banty-weighted and trifling they feel in this large, loud cave they've been forced to go around inside. The nothing now where my mother had been could shock repeatedly, the way a forgetful baby can get blown down when he touches the same ragged light cord each time he crawls by it.

When the door opened now, my mother wasn't the one coming in with groceries and noticing I'd remembered to thaw out the chicken and soak it in milk. She wasn't the one beside me at the Elizabeth Arden counter the day it opened, enticing me to try a little color on my cheeks, nothing heavy, something sheer. Laura was the wrong person doing the right things, and even on days when I almost forgot and it barely mattered that her hair was thick, black, and long, rather than short in brown waves, that she was strong-boned instead of frail, there was no way to forget or correct the fact that I didn't live inside my mother's mind anymore. I wasn't the first and last thought of her day. The hole was emptier than holes with merely nothing in them, it was missing everything that had been possible before. The space was sunk down inside me, like the raw, gouged place there had been in her chest, where her heart was taken out and worked on and then slipped back down and sewn into her a few weeks before the pills she swallowed made it beat so rapidly it couldn't bear the strain and finally, quietly quit.

I went around like a person wearing the wrong size shoes, willing to cut toes off or manage with some broken to keep carrying what my mother did and still walk with a posture that wouldn't draw attention. It was an odd, old show, never stopping to take the shoes off because I stayed so fixated on changing myself instead of them. You realize your method of being in the world isn't a mindless habit. You can do better, but there never seems to be the proper moment to halt everything and get the shoes off and go on forward, so you push on with working. You do not get caught being the old, odd vampire girl on your road.

You're one of those people who have to prove they deserve to be kept on at the countinghouse, and you can be too tired to think but you'll do it, do it again and keep doing what you have to do because you're also too scared of being marked off to stop. And at the end of the day, you go home with the proof of your labors, and she's glad to see someone who's always so willing to do everything precisely and create such large, perfect portions. In a universe they claim is unfolding just as it should, I believe you'll survive and be fine if you know better than to be ruthless and are ashamed to be greedy. You may not be capable of slowing down, but you can manage to look around and be grateful for the day on your rapid way through it.

Five

YOU THINK SMART MEANS WISE.
Then you hope it will soon. This past
autumn, I ran along two parallel lines of
wanting more ease and keeping myself
endangered of strict consequences for
selling poetry. After I branched out on
Martha's tip and word got across to the
high school as well as to the Apocalypse
school, money began coming in so hand
over fist that the fear of going to the
poorhouse if I went to Baltimore

changed into a let-them-eat-cake ease. Clothes to wear up there began flying off layaway. You merely had to take out the savings passbook on the college tuition account I halved the profit into and check the interest compounding to remember the rewards of labor and thrift.

Caught up, I ignored common sense saying to deposit less into the college fund and have more time for the camp, and when they sent a bill for what I owed after the scholarship figure was discounted out, it was either shortchange the future, borrow from Laura, or stay home. I went up there owing her two hundred dollars, a drop in the bucket on the overall costs, but enough by itself to roil through your system at night like Ebenezer's crumb of disturbing bad cheese, so I continued on with the poetry industry, at home, on the bus, on the low wall outside school, anywhere I could find to focus with the ghosts of broke pasts hovering over me.

If you felt strained by English, you could choose a precomposed poem for two dollars or get a custom-made one for four. Concrete poetry ran at least a dollar higher. Sonnets would've been five if they'd been assigned, but Mrs. Delacroix said teachers didn't because it was equal to requiring students to explain the hydrogen bomb and it wasn't worth the frustration to dwell on outsized skills at a school that excused you two days off a year to get in hay and kill hogs on your farm.

Twenty of the poems that made up a separate selection book, entitled Meditations on Life Passing You By, came in a flat rush while I was on the way to Baltimore, trying to keep everything about the trip from getting out from under me. When the train pulled away from our station, I had to crawl over a lady to wave out the window at Laura, Stuart and his mother, Starletta and her mother who'd come by to say Study hard, make friends, we'll be here when you get back. When I made it back to my seat I was too edgy to read and too knotted up to eat even a salted cracker out of my box lunch. Before I knew it, I'd started getting up and down and attracting looks to where I wanted to tell people, I'm just overwhelmed is all.

The lady looked at me like she wanted to ask me whether my mother had packed me with some kind of pill but instead she asked where I was headed, and I told her I was going to learn about how artistic things compare and contrast with science. God knows how much time I'd chewed up wondering things like how somebody first put math and moods together in iambic pentameter, the truth of van Gogh's ear issue, why so many great geniuses have bad wrecks for lives, for example, how Poe was full of a lust for life yet crippled by his appetites and jealousy.

She said, Where are you going to do that?

In Baltimore, I said, where Poe finally

threw up his hands and fell, on a walking tour. Speaking of which, I wouldn't mind hitting my shoes with the polish a time or two more before we get there. I'll be right back.

I'd gone by Laura's old etiquette book for advice to young ladies traveling alone by rail because going to Baltimore on a train had a 1958 tinge to it. I'd used what Martha's twin high school brothers had paid for two themes on the meaning of I Must Go Down to the Sea Again, and the bonus for making twin work different enough for the saddle oxfords. I realized while I was breaking them in I'd need to rest my feet in my sneakers but the porter said people don't go back into their belongings once they're checked in. I was going to ask the lady if she'd ask him on my behalf and explain I wasn't planning to get in the baggage compartment and ramble, but when I got to my seat, she'd given it up to another lady she said was a friend, though they couldn't have been better strangers.

I got my satchel and purse from the overhead, saying I thought seats were assigned in first class and knowing she'd say there were a dozen more and she and her buddy had to catch up, the way things unfold like a story that wastes your time when you know the plot and symbols by rote. The porter said to take any seat available. I had a chapter left in the only book that wasn't packed in the bag he still wouldn't allow me into, so tensing over the destination, cranked up with the thrill of train travel itself, and pitched at a level the gentleman beside me behaved like he didn't want to endure. On the way back over him, I mentioned how I didn't want to end up like a friend of mine who was still nursing blisters from Wolverines and said, Wish me luck on breaking in these hard shoes.

Stuart had actually been the one to rub them with saddle oil the previous

evening, but giving a sales-looking man
a practical reason for my walking up and
down the aisle and crossing over rattling
connections seemed more likely to dis-
courage him from giving away my seat.
I said I'd be back in a minute, but I
found it took a while to check out the
other compartments and see what con-
clusions you can draw about people in
different classes and what the exceptions
were, like if there were wealthy people in
the back class looking like they enjoyed
saving money or people like me in first
class who seemed to be there on a scholarship or gift. After that, I remembered
I'd told Laura I'd see if the berths were
like the ones in Some Like It Hot, but
the woman behind the counter in the
dinette car said unless you sleep reared
back in your chair, this was not a sleeping train.

She kept offering me something to
eat, but you hear too many stories of
young people going somewhere for the
first time and spending all their money

on the way there. I said I didn't care for
anything though her food looked good
despite what I'd heard about them
steaming everything by the engine. She
said that was part of the legend of trains
she could disprove by showing me
where she took foods out of the freezer
box and placed them directly into a
miniature oven. Talking to someone
about her job isn't chatting with the person in the other seat, so I didn't mind
explaining about not wanting to arrive
spent out or about the steam. When we
stopped at Union Station in Washington DC, she said to come in with her
while she picked up her family's pastries
and have a coffee and bagel with her
at a table under the dome to see what
that was like. I can say now that it was
supersaturating without feeling dazey
again, so anyone whose legs are prone
to vibrate when something like the
curved top of the world is revealed,
should hold the rail or sit and allow the
rushers to pass.

I thought I'd talked enough to the dinette woman to be quiet when I sat down again by the man, but when you take off from the station you're blown out of a tunnel into a bright force of light, and I had to say, I apologize, but look at everything outside the window. I can't believe we're moving through it this fast, Mother of God, this is quick. It's like it's moving by you, but it's entirely the opposite and something to think about. If you don't mind me doing it, I'd like to write it down now and not wait and look back in tranquility and probably be wasteful forgetting. What do you think?

He said, I think that'd be fine. You go ahead and do that, but don't hold it against me if I go to sleep.

I told him I envy sleep actually, and when he woke up in Baltimore three hours later he said the breakdown we'd had earlier would make him late for a job meeting. I didn't want to lose the work and he wasn't in the mood or I could've torn him out a poem entitled, On the Road to Nowhere Rapidly. There were twenty-five poems, with an overall theme of carpe diem with a side-line of Beauty. Titling it Meditations on Life Passing You By came from mixing the common sense of how I was watching out the window with the symbolism of how we all should stare out less and seize so much more. Four or five poems became alike when the breakdown stalled the scenery at a very small town with a couple of stores and a few houses. I got over the hump of repeatedly writing how depressed you'd have to be living there by finally writing,

If at First You Cannot Leave

If at first you cannot leave this
    village of woe,
Because you are bound to your
    relatives,

Look outside your window and see,
The train stalled outside your small
    depot,
And ask yourself what's interesting
    about the tracks,
Sit on your low, ragged porches to
    think if you must,
Then hear the whistle,
I heard it,
It blows,
And see the train in the other
    direction, it goes,
I saw it,
It goes,
And if you ask your family what's
    interesting about that,
And they say they have no clue,
Then say your good-byes and grab
    your suitcase,
And walk down your weedy town
    hill to board,
The next train that comes by,
But don't beat yourself up, leaving
    your clan,

For trains that go in one direction
   always come in the other,
And will bring you home again to
   visit dear old Mother.

I'd always counted Baltimore on the Southern side, and I'd expected the other students to hail from places I was used to meeting people from. I had no clue it was going to be more toward Harvard in the habits and ways people brought with them, so there was some rolling stomach panic going on when I realized I had to have conversations with people I hadn't had time to mentally adapt myself to yet. You don't hear how ignorant your accent makes you sound until you have to hear it against other accents, especially when you're competing with people with the edge of the accent that makes them seem like automatic experts.

I decided the trick was to hush entirely or just avoid saying anything they could doubt, but I turned from being more or less confident to thoroughly flabbergasted when I got to the check-in area where chaperones introduce students around, and a clot I had to stand in wanted to know what it was like being a curiosity in a world of nonreaders and racists. I had to leave before the panic began leaking out in balls of forehead sweat or heavy breathing. I knew the truth about where I lived and also how whipped you feel after you try to explain something to people who don't want to change their minds and would never understand how they could be the ignorant ones.

Johns Hopkins had the green quad, the archways, and a mix of modern and stone buildings, and when I followed the map to the dormitory and saw it was not only stone but many gabled, being stunned that I was spending the night in a building like this made it absolutely not matter that the people who'd just behaved like I was lost on the way to mop something up were going to be sleeping in there with me. The way the gables spiked in the sky and how you could imagine finding somebody up there in a dormer room, hunched over with a blanket around his shoulders, possibly coughing with tuberculosis, writing with papers strung and strewed everywhere, I didn't care if they believed their fate included high matters of serious beauty and mine was to ask them whether they had any more silver I need to polish.

I noticed a thin girl with red hair and slippery white skin at the top of the steps, looking at name tags as girls went by her, and then as I passed her, she said, Stop, you're my roommate. I need you to let me in to get my stuff out.

It was addling, but I understood how she so much hadn't wanted to stay with a stranger that she was willing to sleep on the floor in the room with a girl she knew from home. I thought it was also grounds to try to get along, but once we

were in the room, she was out so fast
that I'm not sure if her name was Lola
or Nola. I just thought, Well, more
power to you and arranged my things
around and studied through all the as-
signments we'd been sent for the weekend. I was glad to be around people who
took the same thing that interested me
seriously. But when classes started they
looked set on not finding any pleasure
in it, jumping on you the second you
answered a question. For instance, when
I said Hemingway's stories are an example of where a writer uses a kind of
science of reason to keep the emotions
from getting out of hand, a long-legged
boy in a sweater vest across from me at
the table appeared to have no clue that
you shouldn't ask a stranger, especially a
female, why she didn't see the difference
between reason and brain-damaged
writing.

I said, I don't know. Nobody's ever
asked me that kind of question. I can't
answer it.

The teacher let the boy ask me why, and I said, Because of the way it was put to me.

I fumed through that class and a couple more and finally got to a class I'd been looking forward to that was held walking around in a gallery of photographs of outstanding scenery from the meatpacking plant days of Chicago and the violent early days of trade unions marching in the streets. It occurred to me to ask a teacher, being careful to do it on the side, if people being able to take pictures more conveniently was connected to people starting to write realistically. While I was walking to the library and feeling a great deal of adrenaline over things the teacher had said I should look up about Theodore Dreiser and John Steinbeck, a girl I hadn't noticed overhearing us came up beside me and said, I'm so tired of Sister Carrie I'd puke if I had to read it again.

I told her my teachers at home hadn't

assigned the book yet, knowing it sounded like I went to school in a floored pen, and while I was trying to think of what they could've been preoccupied for us to study instead, she told me she was homeschooled and her mother doted on particular periods and ignored others and it grated on her.

For mercy, she trotted, I imagined, to find somebody else to expose how much she knew to, which was such a running motive there and such a blaring one that any leftover nerves I'd had about Dr. Bok thinking I was a journey-proud brag became concern the letter was too timid and so quiet that it was for all intents and purposes Braille. Being the real thing, I thought, made you confident to say less than you know and not lord information, the kind of hard moral plateaus you shoot for and may sometimes miss. Outside a couple of severe introverts, what I saw said college could be full of characters like the ones who'd crawled in the windows and blistered the calm of Laura's house, only this crowd got a sad charge out of narrating tours of the intellect and museums you hadn't been on and letting you know you weren't the first one to discover something. It didn't matter if a thousand scholars studied how Madame Bovary probably wouldn't have had to rot from the inside if she'd read better books in her girlhood, if the idea strikes you in Baltimore in a room full of people who say they already know, my theory is it's still your personal news.

By the time the librarian worked down the row to me, I didn't need her to explain their card catalog as much as I had to know where they kept the world atlases. She brought an outsized one to a table, and then I pressed my finger down on Baltimore and moved it down, thinking, I'm here, and I want to be there. When I'm there, I'll want to be here again. I was standing by a map of the world in a city I'd never been to, and neither mother could see me, and after I measured from here to there with my fingers, I moved them around west to east, and the distance put me in the middle of the ocean and proved how far out of someone's reach you could get, being pulled backward and pushed forward. Of all the things I'd learned and despite a knack for rapid imagining, I didn't know how to feel at home out in the world or at home either, though all I could think to do next was close the book and wait for a train pointed toward there.

Six

IT TOOK LUTHER AND HIS LONG-lipped cousin to show me the price of what had flown out of the window I'd meditated from. Our bus picked up the cousin from the side of the road and waited while the males pushed his car into a field. When they got back on, the topic moved from what had just blown up under his hood to how his clubs, the Future Farmers of America and the Junior National Rifle Association, were

teaming up to kill enough hogs to fi-
nance an overnight excursion to the
Outer Banks for the Future Homemak-
ers of America club his sisters were in.
Stuart was talking into my ear, but I told
him I needed to listen to how these girls
were going to see the play The Lost Colony, an outdoor drama about the settlers
who became lost trying to establish a
colony under grim circumstances, with
the spotlight on Virginia Dare, the first
little white girl born in the New World.

Laura and I had been planning to go
for a while, and when I leaned up and
asked Luther and his cousin whether it'd
be possible for me to pay and swing a
ride, Luther said, She's the girl I told
you about. Tell her what English you
have due Monday.

I hadn't noticed his facial features because his back had been to me, but
when he turned around with his assignment, I told him I'd look at it and barely
held back asking why he'd hacked off his
bangs to where they couldn't lay flat but

had to dart outward from his head. It was the haircut you most associate with backwoods individuals, no one very bright, but he was organizing the charity donation for the club, so maybe his mother grabbed him with the scissors, very mad, and probably disgusted with his habit of pulling his bottom lip too far out and speaking with the inner-tissue moistness exposed.

Stuart whispered in my hair, Good God, I wish he'd stop. Huh, I'd charge double to have to look at that and write.

He could've been training his lip to have a tribal plate installed, and when he offered to pick up his work, I gave back the assignment, not wanting to spend Saturday dreading Sunday. Luther spoke low and extreme, I told him you keep a stock with you usually, Ellen. You couldn't allowance him out one and do me a favor for him?

He has rhyming couplets due Monday, I told him, on nature, and I don't have any, and the weekend's already

pushed, but anybody who can put together a way to get future housewives to
a drama should be able to knock it out.

The cousin looked over his shoulder,
saying, Never mind. I can draw one off
the English book.

I said, Do what?

Draw, he said, out of the book.

When I asked if he'd ever turned in
work he'd copied from his own book, he
said, Not yet, hadn't had to turn in.

He had the driver let him off at the
bottom of his path, and the summary of
what Luther said was his cousin didn't
understand that the poems in his English book or anywhere else belonged to
the people who wrote them, and if they
could be recited, he didn't see why he
couldn't claim one. Luther couldn't say
how he'd gotten to high school, never
having turned in a piece of creative
work, but he seemed unlikely to stay,
and his mother had asked Luther to
lend a hand after his improved attitude

and attendance had become the talk of their family.

Luther and I got off the bus together, and standing by the ditch, looking at the large cat sleeping in his yard, he said, I tried to tell him what you said to me about this time of year being when you can pick up the beat, but his speed goes from slow to freezing if he has to write something. When he crossed the road though, the teacher said he had to start turning writing in or they'd expel him, which put his mother in a swivet, crying, calling for people to throw in and help him.

I had Luther come in the house and eat a snack or two while he waited on the arm of the chair to tell me if it favored his cousin to say,

Nature

Nature is an old wise owl,
Nature is a bobcat howl.

Nature is the only way,
Birds know where to fly and stay.

Nature's here now when it's cool,
And when you heat to death in
    school.

Nature is what's always around us,
Not in but outside a bus.

Nature will be on my farm of the
    future,
If Nature gets a grade I'm not
    used to.

When Luther said the poem was the image of his cousin and asked how much I wanted for it, I told him I was glad, but nothing. He said, I thought you were going to the fair tomorrow, but since you're dying, I'll tell my mother you need some soup run toward this way over the pasture.

No, I told him, not dying, not drawing poems out of a book or seized frozen either.

If I charge his cousin or anybody else for the one thing I know how to do fairly easily, I'd remind myself too much of the greedy-minded individuals from the classes, but I told Luther only, The people in Baltimore were at another extreme, and I don't see myself going there.

While you were gone, he said, Stuart told everybody you should come home on account of they had a reputation for taking legs.

His great-uncle, I said, lost his leg to diabetes in the hospital up there is all, an amputation, not body snatching.

If it was me, he said, I'd charge Stuart to take him places and be around generally. The way he's been, you wouldn't miss the profit off the poems.

I said, Tell it, and followed him to the door, watching him leave, going along through gold hay pasture. Without someone stepping in to put a frame around the view and heighten what I saw into scenery, it couldn't rise past a boy walking through a field on the side of a narrow road and be called a background. I needed to run behind him, shouting the one good, real and true thing I'd brought home from Baltimore. It felt urgent to announce how there was an individual who once loved humanity so creatively he'd called the place he'd found the Isle of Man. I also had to be struck by how the long-lengthed range of him was so giant-sized compared to the picture of him knocking his heels against a metal grammar grade desk. This tall, this rapid, the world must've been able to see us growing, moving physical upward.

When the school year started, the school nurse measured us together in her room, and there'd been the sensation of old sameness when I saw my percentile marks high on the height chart and in the low-middle on weight. Numbers didn't help me recognize myself as much as the people there with me always had. When Martha, Luther, Stuart, and the rest went through a phase of their heads outgrowing their bodies, things were so jangled that the memory of what I saw in a mirror left when I blinked, but they reminded me that I was a girl, alive and well enough to report to school and stay available to pass through stages with other individuals.

If they smelled like the red, indented kickballs or like crayons, I knew I carried the odor of school on my hands and in my hair and liked to think it was pleasant to people, though now you'll smell Windsong on us, or Aqua Velva and our legs reach out across wide aisles and fields. They've stayed simple to be around, except for Stuart, who turned an interfering, constant longing on me about a year ago, but you behave with some honor around what can seem like foolishness, because he's a mistake waiting to happen with a heart of gold. The night before my mother's funeral, my Aunt Nadine had come and taken all my mother's things from the house, the gold compact mirror, scarves, her brush and comb, pearls, dresses, everything except a pair of stockings, which I wore rolled over and rubber-banded to school and elsewhere beyond that day until the holes were larger than my legs. The morning I returned to school after my mother's funeral, Stuart knew what I needed and gave it to me in a way I could manage. When I reached under my desk, I found a sack of gobbed candy corn, some pocket change, and seven dilapidated dollar bills he'd put in a brown lunch sack with a note to say,

Dere Ellen
I diding lik the candy but I hope you will. Dont eat it all at one time. If you dislik it you can go to the stor for sum you do lik and thow this korn in the trach.
I cooding go to the stor becaws I am in trobel for mizbeehaven on the way home from your mamas funrel yes terday.

I wisseld wen you need to stay quiat after some body is ded. I pollogize. My daddy sed it was dizrespetfull of me and punnsht me and went to the stor by hisself widdout me but he came bak unmad and sed I culd help him shav tonite. He tole me your mama was a nise womn. Yuse the chang to git som nise foods.

This is the longess ledder in the werld for me. I muss stop.

Your frend,

Stuart.

Seven

ON THE WAY TO THE FAIR, I WAS IN the front seat with Laura, reading her a society snippet from the morning paper about how Ava Gardner, who was born a few roads over, had arrived for a quiet family visit, greeted by neatly bib-and-tuckered young kin, who more or less lost their minds, thrilled with the many souvenirs of Spain she'd brought them. When I asked whether she knew what sans Frank Sinatra or bull fighter meant, she said, Without them, but what's that scratching in the backseat? Look around and see if Stuart or Starletta developed hives in their sleep.

The sound came from Stuart's stomach, which from the way he was turned, had some extraordinary lumps I hadn't seen before that had to be causing the noise when his clothes scraped against them. I said, I'd pull his sweater and undershirt up if I didn't still have an eyeful.

It isn't worth it, she said, nothing is.

The nostalgia that kept us from inspecting him came from the summer before when his mother saw my bicycle parked next door and ran inside to pull me out of selling magazines to their profitable neighbor who owned vending machines for a living. She needed me to help her pull Stuart out from where he'd run from her and gotten stuck under his bed in the nude. While she'd been out, her can of instant suntan had accidentally gotten away from him on a white bedspread, after he'd shaved his body so the color would soak in and chopped himself up pretty well in the bathroom. Because he hadn't bled to death yet and he thought his mother was still in town with his little brother Henry, he took his first shave and did some other grooming as well.

We threw him her red robe and pulled him out by the feet, and he came out as such a blow to the system that you could call home the dank under-belly of a city dripping continually and never see anything like it. She yanked the robe closed on him and tied it harder than Luther's mother ties the bobcat to the tree before a vacation. With him afraid to talk, we had no way of knowing why there were frozen green peas packed in his ears until we realized he'd reamed and gouged around with his father's ear trimmer and figured he was trying to freeze the end of his blood vessels. Stuart's mother had me ride Henry to the store in my bicycle basket and let him eat candy, watching to be sure he didn't expose what was happening at home, to give her time to bleach him.

I couldn't account for today's scratching or the odd shape on Stuart's belly, but I knew when I found out, the news was going to be out where Stuart usually reached, and complicated. All week, he'd been promising to bring a hundred dollars to be a gentleman with. When he'd fallen asleep wedged around Starletta, I read Laura the list he'd given me when just after dawn his mother had slowed down her car and rolled him, staggering, into our front yard. I doubted he'd accumulated the money, and he absolutely hadn't found more spelling skills, but he'd been sure to plan.

What I Tend to Do With Ellen and Show Her To

Slingin rides I love to wach but you
    couldnt pay me to ride—Wach
    with Ellen
Childrun tendin there flocks of

sheeps and other barnyeard
animals—Wach with Ellen
Presdents faces painted on eggs,
Stachu of Liburty painted on
eggs—Show Ellen
Peecocks, monkees, Sonny and
Cher, exhotic beests of the jungul
and all made out of everyday
kitchen foods—Show Ellen
Swurl art wher you squrt paint out
of catchup squrt bottles and they
spin it into art—Ellen loves art so
leed her to it
Outsize turkey legs and candeed
apples—Feed Ellen
Mrs. Tom Thum, the Smallest
Woman Alive—Show Ellen
Doan walk off a way from the
grupe, get More Avien cooky,
thank Lora for carrion you, don
get fool into given the shot gun
game man all yure money, don
show off for Ellen to see thu you
and run, get to the bafroom befor
it gets bad—Mama sede

After we'd waited in the traffic line and found a parking place, Laura got out, saying she had one nerve that hadn't been danced on and needed to pull herself together with a bench and a Coca-Cola in a bottle before we were swept away too far inside Gate Five, where we had to give the bag of donated canned goods for free entry. After she dampened a place on her hem and wiped grit crystals from Starletta's eyes, Stuart said his eyeballs felt like they were being cut into as well and stood behind Starletta in line, describing how thick his eye matter could be, particularly after he'd slept in daylight.

Laura fluffed her skirt back down and said, Stuart, you don't have a clear idea of how well you'd have to know a person before they'd love to hear you tell that, do you?

He said, Huh, I was just saying is all.

He pulled out his shirttail and then crammed it back in, saying, Nothing, nothing, huh, let's get rolling.

Rolling toward the gate, with him a little ahead of us and sloped completely over, weighted down by the three sacks of cans he'd insisted on carrying, he banked off cars now and then, more off his axis than normal. Starletta doesn't know how heavy she is, and each holding her by a hand, Laura and I heard our shoulders pop when she'd jump and lunge forward. We didn't so much roll as we jerked to the gate. Stuart still looked too lumpy around the middle, but he'd begun walking more and more upright, like the ape to human evolution picture, and while Laura watched him turn in the cans for us, she said, He has some very strange conduct. Is his mother going to allow them to issue him a driver's license?

I couldn't tell her everybody dreaded it because he was there with the tickets, saying, I need to find a bathroom to have any money.

Laura said, Tell me why that is, son. I'm interested.

He told her, It got to where I kept saying I needed to bring a hundred dollars and pave the way for everybody and my mother kept saying I didn't. But you know the man that owns the vending machines that has the house next to me? I took all my and Henry's change and what was in some jars and coats and different places to get him to turn it into dollars, but all he had was quarters, so I said that was fine, and then I remembered what a man on a show did with some duct tape and dynamite one time, so I got home and took care of it so I didn't have to wake up with it to do this morning.

So, she said, you need to go to the restroom and, well, unbind a hundred dollars in quarters from yourself that you slept in.

Yes mam, he said, and even though it's only sixty, I'm still afraid it could hurt. Do you have any lotion with you? Ellen can tell you it's not a story to say I've got sensitive skin.

It always hurts less when you pull tape off yourself, I told him. Just go do it quick and have it be over with. Starletta's about to start spinning, and the next stop can't be the Red Cross tent.

He was gone long enough for us to visualize him sitting in a stall with duct tape stuck to his hands and his pink skin flaming, so Laura stopped a man at the door and asked him, Do you mind handing this tube of lotion to the little big-boned boy in there for me? His name's Stuart, if you don't see him, call him.

Stuart finally came out, glad for the lotion though now with his shirt sticking to him, saying, Okay, ladies, I'm ready to motorvate.

We changed four sandwich bags of quarters into bills and bought all the ride and show tickets we needed for the day. We stopped at the Village of Yesteryear first to find the Moravian booth and have the rest of the day without the pressure of remembering his mother's cookies, which come canned, so there's no breakage in a satchel. The booth was along a rim of other booths and small areas where they displayed folk customs and crafts, so Stuart and I kept Starletta with us while Laura looked at quilts.

People visit the Moravian ladies' booth in droves for the thin ginger cookies they bake on the premises, and although they're high, if you decide it's too much to ask, you'll wait a year because when the fair closes, they pack up the ovens and journey back to their own world in the western part of the state. They can be compared to the Amish in many of the ways they carry on their affairs, but they contrast on accepting the modern car and the electricity that enables them to have the kind of massive baking operation they were running that morning.

Starletta had on a yellow plaid waisted dress with a green belt, white fold-down ankle socks and blue tennis shoes, and you could tell she'd struggled against her mother believing that colored girls need to go out matching more than most and had won on the dingy striped sweater she took off and tied around her shoulders when she got overheated sucking cookie crumbs up out of what appeared to her as a convenient trough on the side of the Moravian table. I told myself the Moravian lady glaring like I'd wound Starletta up and turned her loose would end once Stuart made his purchase, but Stuart's beading sweating and mumbling told everyone in the booth to come get a load of this boy. Stalled, frustrated, he asked me, Ellen, how many pounds is it to the can? Mama said three pounds, but the label says it's so many ounces to the can.

If he can keep to a rhythm he knows well, he's fine, but off it, he suffers, and worse in public, when he must feel so much farther away from his father, who he craves to be in charge of him on the few days a month he's not away tracking down rubber. The last time his father

was home, he told me Stuart had outlined a future with me, saying to please
be careful of Stuart's tenderhearted emotions until they passed and also stay safe,
avoiding offers to go out in his raft. In
fact, he told me I should turn down any
invitations that involved his son and
fire, outside the rubber pile, experiments
with kites in thunderstorms, fishing off
the bridge or in their canoe, and overall,
any open body of water.

A Moravian lady refilled the crumb
tray to see what Starletta would do, and
about the time she was down into it
hard with both hands to scoop, I said,
Stuart, we need to get out of here. Get
three cans and let's go.

He took out his billfold, and had me
turn from the table while he whispered
in my ear, Is what she's cramming in
free? I bet she's tooken five pounds. I'll
get the three for home and one for each
of us, so that's, huh, seven. It sounds like
too much to carry though, but, huh, I'll
take your satchel.

That's very thoughtful, I told him, but you ought to let that be it and not worry about paying for other things during the day. We didn't come expecting it, so offer to repay the lady on Starletta while she's making out the ticket, and she'll say never mind it, so that'll be all.

Stuart took it in and told the lady, I'd like to go ahead and, huh, give you what you take for seven cans, if you'll let me, and see if I mighten ought to get straight with you on the samples.

He sounded like an old country man, ordering at a sit-down restaurant, because it was how he knew to be right then, and you could tell the lady knew it. She didn't have to stop Starletta by taking the tray up and rush cleaning, and she didn't need to refuse to tell him the price and make him stand there with his billfold open while she finished sizing us up as being the overscrubbed little colored girl with the hundred plaits and plastic bows in her hair, shoving in pricey crumbs she couldn't have at home because welfare didn't pay for sugared snacks anymore. She saw the sweaty, pumpkin-headed boy in husky corduroy pants and a hot-looking boiled-wool jacket with both shoes overflowing with bandaging he'd thought ahead to prevent blisters with. To her mind, neither he nor the colored girl had been anywhere, unlike the girl between them, who'd been to some places and learned how not to look like a tourist, conceited enough to have chosen clothes to make her look slightly above the grime and grist, and also quick-eyed the way tight situations teach you to be. That surprised her, I could tell by the way she looked at me and kept Stuart needing. I was standing there just as dumbstruck as he was.

I couldn't move for the wall I hadn't expected to find that day, at least not so early and at a religion's booth. If Laura didn't swoop in soon, I saw myself leaving some figure of money on the table with the kind of note you imagine writing to people who absorb the day-to-day bravery you need to get around with, saying, You're in a costume, taking money from strangers at the fair. What harm would it do to be decent? You have a bad grease stain on your left chest. Hide and watch it come out in the wash.

Before I saw Laura with her hands on Stuart's shoulders, I heard her say, There's so much clang and clatter in here, so let's make this quick. Let's say what's owed and bag it, but I need one extra can, please.

She paid and then opened the can and poured the cookies out onto the sampling tray, saying, We're even now. You think?

We didn't talk on the way out, and before we got back in with the stream of people, Stuart had us stop so he could take Starletta's pumpkin pin off her collar and switch it to her skirt so she could handle it without her chin to her chest, running into people. Then standing up, he told Laura, The lady had mean coming to her, huh, you burned her.

She said, I didn't tell her to have a nice day is all, as you say. It sounds rude to omit what people know to be a lie, but you didn't need to carry her out in the satchel.

Starletta was drawn toward where a migrant-looking boy was calling out for fresh swirl artists at his booth, so we all kept the color bottles directed while she squirted with her eyes closed and then became so fixated watching them swirl that although her eyes were opened, the boy said, The little girl, she sleep on her feet.

Stuart said a Methodist hot dog would wake all our moods up, and when Laura and I didn't know what they were, he tapped his back pocket and said, I swear before God, I'd love to introduce you to one.

They were unusually juicy, and while Laura went across to buy a football team

hand towel to tie around Starletta, Stuart said, You know the taxidermy booth?
The reason I know so much about out
here is Luther and Harvey and me spent
the night in it last year and it was next
to the Methodists then so when they
closed up, they allowed us to take ten,
fifteen for a constellation prize after
Luther worked like he did on the rac-
coon and had the letdown when they
wouldn't let him run something that
wild and not know if it had been rabid
or not.

What was he supposed to stuff, I said,
a dog? His father had wolves riding
around in their old car, drying with the
top down.

He was still explaining something
about a mysterious film the judges had
seen on the animals' eyes when we'd all
left to walk down the main way, eating,
with Starletta switching her narrow tail
and looking fast and terrific, chewing
without the bib Laura couldn't put on
her, and looking up to follow the voice

she knew belonged to the weatherman. The closer we got to the television tent, the more you heard women's voices, saying he's good-looking but not striking, he's secretly married, he's too tan and his suits fit too much like rubber, his face looks rubber, embalmed, reading aloud off the information tables about how he boasts a master's degree in science and loves to cook and fly radio control airplanes.

We stood for Starletta to meet him with some women who seemed to be dreaming of how they'd insert him onto their sofas and discard the men who were leaning against the tent poles to wait. When I edged Starletta to the side of the line for a better view of him signing autographs, she cut out and found an alley between two tents to stand and look petrified in.

I told Laura you couldn't predict it, but her mother said this happened when Starletta recognized a salesman from his used car lot commercials and squatted to hide in fear beside a car. She'd thought the weatherman would be sized to fit the television set. She came out when we told her we'd go to the pick-up ducks booth next, the most luring thing she'd go along with, and then we stayed there through twenty dollars and noon. In the midst of corrupted nastiness of unfair games and people in public with threatening sayings on their shirts, we fell under a spell of mesmerization, watching the ducks streaming by, and when I felt Starletta's wet hand on mine, I fell deeper in to wonder if she understood what her body was making mine remember, my mother's hand on mine, under warm, soapy water, searching around for the chain on the stopper after we'd washed combs and brushes on Saturday mornings. When we were ready to go and waiting for Starletta to fit her fingers out with prize rings, Laura asked what was the matter, and Stuart said, Huh, I think you look patriotic.

I said I'd be fine, but I'd prefer taking

the long walk to the slow rides and miss the sights of the slinging ones. It's another kind of ambition that makes you consent to be strapped down on the edge of a rickety circle and slung around to yell like you're glad to be there. I don't scream except in shock or squeal over anything pleasing. I enjoy the sharp pleats on the high school cheerleaders' uniforms, and I like it that our pack of rural girls can flip around and keep the pace in time, but no matter how hard they shout to shout back and go through their set of large arm motions with them, I have to stand there, remembering to smile and clap at the end, hoping it looks like the planet that assigned me to observe this pep rally has rules against me getting whipped up in the action. If startling jolts and frenzy could be eliminated, I could almost be comfortable, the way people with reptile phobias must feel more relaxed living in Ireland. I wasn't as afraid of shooting straight down from a wild ride as I was of my seat cracking off the spoke and shooting me out over the fair. If you've had it happen before with things jerking and shaking off the rails and speeding up before you were thrown outward, you don't acquire a deliberate ticket on centrifugal force.

Starletta rode around on several small, quiet circles, and then Stuart narrated us around the exotic carved and molded food creations in the food building, not saying what he knew, but what he wished he knew about how the things were formed, and when he fixed on a lard replica of Iwo Jima, which had won, he said, Huh, now that's a hobby. You ready to go see Mrs. Thumb?

Laura said she wasn't, so she took Starletta to meet us there later, going off one way while we went the other, irritating long way toward the oddity and striptease rows. Starletta's mother had told me she heard they keep them so far to the edge because the Bureau of Agriculture leader in charge of organizing it had a loud civic wife who drew the fair plan on a napkin.

Nothing's worth this, I told him. She'd better not be on her knees in a long dress.

He stopped walking and blurted, If you think you're better than people like Mrs. Thumb, can you try to hide it harder so I can have a good time?

Stuart, I said, I never know what to do when you decide to let me in on an argument you've been having for us.

He said, But don't tell me you weren't thinking what I said.

Some of it, I told him. I'd be ashamed to tell Starletta's mother we inspected people like slavery.

He said, I knew you'd dislike it in one way, but the other way, I thought you would because you go for unusual things. It's confusing to be walking along, not knowing if you're going to make me like it or despise it. You behave better than me and I'm the one that knows your aunt and cousin are moving

somewhere the first of November because Dora's expecting.

When he said the news came from
his mother and was beginning to circu-
late around, I said, You should've let me
find out random so I wouldn't attach it
to you.

I know, he said, but I swear before
God, Ellen Foster, you take a great deal
out of people. You want to see her or
not?

I asked, Mrs. Thumb or my aunt?

Both, he said, I supposed I imagined.

I said, I can't think to tell whether I
have a choice on either, but we're almost
in the oddity zone.

When you'd mention what you
wanted or didn't want around my father,
he'd say to spit in one hand and wish in
the other one to see which one got full
first, to forgive himself for having nothing to do with how things could turn
out for you. Spit would roll through my
fingers before anything I wished about
my aunt was accomplished. No one was

going to hold my Aunt Nadine down while I screamed over my mother's missing things. No one could hold the universe down until it explained why my life had been this particular one and how the rest of it could happen without work taking over and being a secret insanity I'd have to keep hidden to get along in ordinary ways, and particularly in case a man I might love would have me. Males lean toward females with better histories, and although it would be ideal, it would be a rare thing to find one who wouldn't say my history's too freakish for his taste and move on.

Waiting in a long ticket line, I wasn't sure whether I wanted more to leave the misery or injure the people who'd forced me to be inside it more. We didn't mind running to Mrs. Thumb's house with the tickets because the line had drained our time down to a few minutes before the hour, but when we got there blowing, the people coming down her steps said none of the human and animal shows had a set time. You showed up and looked in on her daily life and stayed until she ran you off. When our turn came to group around the short door, she was sitting on her sofa flipping through a True Story magazine with her bare feet propped on one of the stuffed Dalmatians you win throwing darts nearby, fuming.

Stuart whispered, She's got painted toenails. Look, her feet look like the knotted cedar they make lamps out of.

She slammed the magazine down in her lap and said, You talk to your wife like that?

It was sickening to hear the boy's tone when he'd said human and animal shows, but I kept looking because it felt interesting and I had to, despite what Starletta's family from another century had no doubt been put through on slave examining blocks, and what kind of impression I would've made on a human being in the market for another human being.

I touched Stuart's arm and told him never to tell Starletta's mother we were stooped in this door. Stuart was telling Mrs. Thumb, They must take you to the beauty shop every so often, not that you need it though. I was just thinking, huh, everybody's got to get out the house sometimes. It couldn't be healthy, to be shut up. I see you have a fireplace. They keep the chimley working for you?

She glowered at us and twisted around to stand up, so I thanked her for having us, but as we hit the bottom step, we heard her rumbling to the door and shouting, Nope, nope, nope. You didn't stay long enough to leave and not buy something first.

That's okay, I told her. We're fine.

Pulling some pictures out of a low mailbox by the door, she said, I know you are, growny girl, but you don't want your husband to feel guilty for not buy-ing you a picture of me and President Nixon, autographed, a dollar. I don't think he'd want Mrs. Thumb going hungry, so how about bringing me a couple of Methodist hot dogs?

Stuart stepped up and reached a dollar to her and took the picture, saying, I appreciate it. What would you like on your hot dogs?

I said they must have people who come by with lunch and things of that nature, but she said, Nope, they don't deliver out here.

Stuart asked though not with much zest, What could you call for if they did?

After she said she'd take two with mustard and ketchup, slaw, onions, pickle relish, and chili, it shouldn't have felt like news but it did when she listed what she wanted to go with them, French fries, a large grape soda, two candy apples, and an elephant ear. She didn't offer money, which Stuart chalked up to her not knowing the correct amount, but waiting for her order at the variety foods booth, I looked at the picture and told him, I think we just bought Mrs. Thumb a free lunch.

For mercy, Laura's knack of knowing what to do about hard adults was working well enough to attract her and Starletta to be waiting on the bench in front of Mrs. Thumb's house when we got back overloaded. Looking like it wasn't anything she'd ever believe, she said, When I asked the lady if she'd seen you, she said two bright young people had offered to go pick up her lunch, and I could sit over here and wait, and look at a photograph of her and Richard Nixon. I'll take the food in to her. How much does she owe you?

Thanks, I said, this was about all the Hansel and Gretel ordeal I could take.

We stood on the porch with Starletta while Laura hunched around inside the house, making sure the foods were in Mrs. Thumb's reach, and when she noticed a picture of Mrs. Thumb and Richard Burton on the wall, she said, Nixon, not my type, Burton, definitely, but how did you become such a celebrity?

Not aware we were outside the door
or not caring, she said, chewing, Not
one. Have a nephew, does put-together
pictures for a living.

Laura smiled and said, Well, it's good
to have something to make up for everything, and I'm sure lunch would go a
long way if I wasn't going to need five
dollars for it. Do you keep your money
in a particular place? Can we locate that
now and get this taken care of?

Laura came out and handed me five
dirty dollars, and after she'd asked Stuart to stop repeating, We got tooken, she
said, We'll go around some more, but
this day will come to a close only after
Starletta's looked at some sheep, or
goats, and a couple of other very plain,
nonverbal things.

After Stuart said he'd love to go now,
I said, You don't know how fine that is
by me, and I know I need to be extremely nonverbal right now, but I have
to tell you what Stuart told me about
my aunt moving with my cousin some-

where on account of she's pregnant. What am I supposed to do about it?

Nothing, she said, but find Starletta something slow to pet.

I said, But we need to stop a minute. I don't know if this news can get chopped off like the Moravian lady.

Looking at her neck now because she'd turned her face to the sun and interrupted me to tell Starletta she should try it, which made Stuart look up and leave me with three disinterested throats. I said, Laura, you need to look and let me say I meant what I heard about my aunt and cousin is close to being a bulletin from this other world I had to be in for a while, and I've learned it's scheduled to go to another part of the universe and take some very important stuff of mine with it.

She said, But what we should do, Ellen, is have the remainder of the day here without borrowing interruptions. I know you're eager to talk about it, and we can in a little while. I'm only suggesting you take advantage of the peace we came to walk around in some to recover from the hoopla.

I said, I'll try, but we can't postpone delving again. We could delay Dora if we had to because it isn't like I can do anything but wonder who the father is, whether she's going to finish her education, how her mother's treating her, things like that, but I can't wait and let them permanently steal the belongings of my mother's they took from me. I can't let that happen.

It won't, she said, but nothing's happening now except us walking to the pastured barn area.

I told her I'd like to look for the demonstration cow I'd seen in the paper when he was a feature in the veterinary barn last year. He wasn't there, but the summary is he had hi-fi-speaker-looking circles in the side of his body that monitored his digestive track, but the last thing we saw that afternoon was what a

vet told me was the cow's capable replacement. Without saying where the
cow went, he motioned toward a clean
floored pen with a sign on the gate that
said,

Meet Susan!
1974 Medical Miracle
Bovine Research Leads the Way
Support Our Vietnam Vets!
Vets for Vets!

From what her keeper described to
us, the farmer who owned Susan took
her to the veterinary school because she
had a place that was found to be cancer
in what would be our thigh. There appeared to be no way to save her, but
then a surgeon said he could try something different if the farmer was willing.

I said, Which he had to be, of course.

Yes, he was willing to do what it took,
so Susan got her surgery as volunteer to
have the section of her leg with the place
on it removed and replaced with a me-

chanical leg section. She has an improved ability to go around in the pen and small pastures and though she hobbles, you think, anybody would and all the best to her regardless.

Eight

ON THE WAY HOME, THE CHOICE was talk to Laura about the only two leftover members of my family leaving and taking all my mother's things with them or put myself to sleep with the droning tires, so I slept and didn't wake up until Stuart was staggering out of the car the way he'd staggered in. As level as Laura was, if the news had been news to her, she would've shown it. She'd known and had time for it to go through her

system to where if you could look into
her like the vets looked into the cow
through her hi-fi-speaker-looking-deal,
the view would've been of calm, eased,
normal flowing.

Starletta's mother needed to know
about Dora and Nadine. I doubted she
did. As much as she was looped into
what took place on our road, people like
Stuart's mother didn't phone up colored
women with gossip. When Starletta's
mother came to pick up Starletta with
her car and new driving license, Laura
and I looked over both the way you
do and then came in to round up Starletta and her fair things from my room.
I told them, I need to know something
first though and what I'm supposed to
be doing about it.

Starletta's mother sat on the tall stool
by the kitchen window Laura uses to
smoke menthol cigarettes out of, with
me thinking, She may want to light one
up now. Sitting at the table, Laura said,
What Ellen's talking about is this busi-

ness Stuart told her, understanding his mother's the source of truth, about Ellen's Aunt Nadine moving to Texas with her daughter, who's pregnant.

While I was rolling back through Stuart's words, searching for Texas, Starletta's mother said, I hope Ellen's going to get everything Nadine took of Shine's before they go.

Laura opened her mouth to let out what she knew about it but stopped when I sat down by her to say, Texas? He didn't say a specific state.

Ellen, she said, it doesn't matter what I knew or didn't. I don't care to count angels.

Starletta's mother opened the narrow cabinet and felt around for the Kools she and every other woman on the road knew were there, saying, The trick is the angels are on Ellen's pin.

I cracked a window while Laura lit the cigarette that landed on the table and said, What am I supposed to do for relief?

Nothing, Laura said. I'm managing this.

Managing to get throat cancer, I told her. You can smoke one a week and fall to it, but this time when I hit the road, it'll be the highway to Texas. I suppose I could nursemaid Dora's baby and crank my old Cinderella lifestyle back up, although if they're hauling my mother's things with them, I can pick a lock and sit in a Texas attic and heatstroke out while I handle them.

When Laura said, The truth is not so bad, Ellen, that you need to create a story and worry yourself with it.

Starletta's mother said, Then tell her the story. And tell me, I'm interested.

Okay then, she said, so your cousin was running with some . . .

Criminals is what I heard, Starletta's mother broke in.

Probably to get attention, I said.

And, Laura said, she ends up pregnant, and that's all I heard for a while, from Stuart's mother.

She dotes on untimed expectancies, I said, so this is fairly typical for her. Unless Dora murdered her mother and replaced her with a pod person twin, she's still under her mother's same thumb, so you feel one way and another about her having something of her own.

She could've gotten knocked up in the unconscious, Starletta's mother said. It wouldn't be the first time a girl let herself loose with the panty girdle.

Laura smiled, saying, Tell Ellen what you're going to study when you start with the college courses next summer.

Social work, she said, but if I told them I've been with Ellen Foster all her life, I'm sure they'll want to graduate me right away, especially after I hear Laura say what the story is on your family this time.

Another cigarette flew to Laura, but she only rolled it around and stared at it until she looked at me and said, So, I didn't say anything about your cousin because I didn't want to stir all that around, not after you'd just mailed everything to Harvard, and we were working on, well, you have difficulty taking things.

Starletta's mother wet her cigarette out in the sink and threw it away, saying, She's right on that, Ellen, like the AA crowd, one thing at a time.

When Laura motioned for her to pull out the chair beside me, like she could use a person closely present, I said, I know my father's brother died last year, and everybody else is dropped off the face, and Stuart's mother stays out of her mind, but she wouldn't be trading gossip with a ghost, so that's it for people left to die. The ordeal list is down to I'm adopted or my father's alive and married to a striptease, or maybe Starletta's my sister, and I'm way light, or my aunt broke the news that I'm an octoroon on her way out of town, which means paving my way stops being a fight, and I notify the United Negro College Fund.

Laura said, I know, Ellen, there's a world of possibility, twists, and hard angles, but it's straightforward, or would be, if anything before you came here wasn't so loaded, I mean.

Heavy, Starletta's mother said, and you're still sore-armed from carrying everything damaged.

Yes, Laura said, but you see, I called your aunt when I heard about the move and told her to get your mother's things together while she was packing the house, and I'd come by for them. I believed that would end it. She said she'd get some boxes together, but she needed to bring them to you, and it would take a week or so. I said you didn't need it, and if she didn't want me at her house, she could take them to Martha's store, or Starletta's, or even her lawyer's office, if she was anxious about anything valuable in it. So she and her daughter are coming, soon, and I was trying to find a way to prevent you going through that.

I was thinking this was too much

vanishing, and if I didn't see my mother's sister, my arms would always have the feeling of a tight need to grab her and make her apologize to me. When Starletta's mother nodded her head down like a prayer and then lifted her eyes up and sighed, I knew she would say what I needed in my life.

Laura, she said, I understand, but Ellen may need a say, not a showdown, just the chance to say a few words and know they were heard. You and I know she spends a great deal of time in her mind, and she may feel due a chance to open it to an individual that stands for all the other individuals that put so much pain in there.

I was trying to arrange some way for you to avoid it, Laura said. That was going to be my job this week, but if you want to see your family, tell me. Keep in mind though the damage if you picture a tender moment or some weepy apology.

Starletta's mother said, I think what

happened blows through Ellen's mind fairly regularly.

It stayed, I said, and you know I wouldn't put my hands to her any way she'd enjoy.

Nadine is a cruel wreck of a white woman, Starletta's mother said, and she deserves to be shaken, but she was Shine's sister. She and her mother went berserk because they couldn't watch Shine dying, slipping down, over so much time and them not able to get her out from inside it to safety. They came out of the funeral home swinging with Ellen in the way, and I'm not saying they shouldn't have stopped and said she's Shine's and taken her, because they should've, but Shine wasn't an ordinary person, Laura. She wasn't like you or me. She fairly glowed, and you watch a light like that go out, and it will absolutely drive you to Satan for help fixing revenge. But strip all that away, and this is still Ellen's family.

When I was little, I believed that tears

formed one at a time and rolled over my eye ledge, and closing my eyes had to be enough to make them stay back. Glad not to see, hearing was adequate when Laura said, But she's my family, you see, I was here, keeping the house filled, my mother gone, father gone long before her, right here where they left me. And this girl came to me, you see, I didn't believe it, at Christmas, and I didn't know if she was real, you know, because of the way there's something so large about her, and what you say about the glowing of Shine's nature, well, the girl glowed too. And what she told me was so goddamn horrifying, walking up here from her aunt's house, but she was here, and I have been so honored she stayed. I've pulled myself out of many blue days just by saying I must be all right, there must be something right about me, if a person this rare and good chose me.

Taking her hand, I told her, I did, I will.

And you will, she said, do the most

amazing things, and what I do, I mean, my life has been keeping a circle around this house, and I can't tolerate the thought of it being broken by anyone who does not wish you well.

When Starletta's mother's said everyone knew what Laura had done, how she'd done what other people couldn't or wouldn't, she was starting to say how the court wouldn't allow her and her husband to take me, and Laura looked at her, not listening, saying, We had a peg-leg man come and build a library. We've waited for box-top packages to arrive from Battle Creek. We've traveled. We've written to Liberace. I'm on this road it'd kill many people to live on. They'd drop from boredom, but I never thought my life would ever be this interesting. Doing nothing with the child can keep me fascinated and content, and nobody who has done that for me, glad to do it, not aware, is going to be subjected to treachery, you know, that manipulative evil her aunt thrives on

without an ounce of guilt, entirely corrupted. I'd blow up the road that runs
by here before I'd let anybody get on it
to come here with a mind to finding any
redemption or doing Ellen any more
damage. There's a circle around this
house, and anybody who doesn't wish
her well has to cross me to get to her,
and these are people, a family, allegedly,
and I'm her mother now, and I think
there's been a goddamn enough. Okay?
Is it plain? Was I heard?

She said she was going to lie down
and not wait for answers, and after Starletta's mother sat in my room and played
with Starletta on the floor, she got up,
saying, You understand you're finally
lucky, right?

I said I hadn't known, and she said I
did now, and to stay to myself and let
Starletta and her run to the meat
counter and bring back a cold supper.
She said, I'll lay out some meats and
cheese before I go home, and I'm telling
you, it's going to feel like a funeral house

around here for a day or more, whether there's pickup food on the table or not. If they sold flowers, I'd buy those, too. I imagine you know what reverent means. You need to be reverent. You need to stay still as you can, and I don't care if you have to imagine it real like these people believing wonders work in coffee grounds and clouds, or fix it like a story you'd write, but you have got to believe a woman who'd blow up the road and die for you had to be sent by Shine. So rest in here with a book to read and let this be a quiet house.

It wasn't possible for the house to be anything but hushed and lowered in the atmosphere though not like after a death. I knew it too well, the way I'd felt when I'd go into a house to sell magazines and be told I should come back in a few days, and knowing without being told that someone is in the back badly fevered or crying. You could tell when you walked in Stuart's house and found him making his brother a sandwich on a paper plate, being careful to use the trash can, that his mother was being tormented by moods her revolving hormones created and used to take her over with. I'd crack open her door to see if she needed anything, and she wouldn't be phoning around gossip or rambling through her purse for something in the second household she claimed to be running in there. She'd be on her side, staring at the window, not seeing anything out of it, and not quite seeing me when she'd say, Nothing, but thank you, I'm fine.

I didn't open Laura's door the rest of the evening, but I did in the morning, and when I asked if she didn't want to take off more than her shoes, knowing her stockings were twisting around her, and get under the top cover at least, she turned her pillow over for the cool side and told me thank you but she was fine. Starletta's mother hadn't said to clean, but it was Saturday morning, which is what we did, and when I took out the products and rags and waited, Laura not coming out was like the woman in the movie who's waiting for the man at the depot, and when one train after another comes without him on it, she has to decide whether to fill out a missing persons report or throw her hands up and start up another love.

I went through the front of the house, my room, and since not running the vacuum cleaner or doing the back rooms created extra time before American Bandstand, I cleaned the car from the fair and outlined what to say to Dr. Bok about how I'd gotten ahead of myself and probably should stay home for now. I'd meant to have it ready for the mailman, but he came while I was inside the car, with nothing but the box of sample magazines. I bathed and crawled onto the sofa with them, not wanting to read anything that would excite ideas enough to break through a time I'd sworn I'd keep quiet.

Starletta's mother called, saying she

was sorry to make the phone ring, and I told her I was as well on account of it went off like a shot. I asked if it was all right to slip a note under Laura's door to remind her about a new comedy show coming on late that night, something we'd emphasized not missing. She said it was fine but leave it at that, and if Laura got up to make supper, help around the edges, but don't treat her like an invalid and take over. She suggested fresh air, so I rode the cookies I'd found in the car down to Stuart's house, but no one was home, so I sat on his bucket and poked at the rubber pile and rode back home, and when I opened the door, I saw what Laura meant when she said we'd made something whole. It would've been whole if every gorgeous thing had been hauled away while I was out, and the air in there would've felt this right weight of solid, because, I knew now, it was made of the air we breathed there.

It would've made the next days easy if I'd believed I'd wanted my mother's things only to touch my hands to what had been inside of rooms she and I were in, when my father was absent, and the air felt like this. I could've told Laura I agreed that my aunt didn't need to come, so don't let her, and if you don't get my mother's belongings, let them go on to Texas, but I wanted them in my hands. And I wanted them in case I had a girl to come open the door of my room to ask if I needed anything, and I'd have the capability to tell her I needed her to sit on the side of the bed while I gave her some small belonging of my mother's. There's life in things. There's life in everything. My mother won't be there to give my girl her heart, and I know she would, so I'll have to. I'll have to do what my mother would've done, say what she would've said, Come here and let me show you something, this is what I have for you because I love you.

I wanted to remember my mother telling me she loved me. She did, you know she did, but I couldn't hear the words. Laura had said everything around it, so had I, though if I'd said it, until now, it would've been a lie. I loved her being there, loved watching her, and I loved that she didn't seem to have a history, how she seemed to have been invented the day I walked into the house. I loved that she was a woman who hid women from laundry and loud boys in their houses, and I loved how she once calmed Starletta's aunt when she came to help us get ready for new kitchen cabinets and brought along her infant who was wailing, hungry, but her mother was too jazzed, she said, by some nasty life events that had taken place right before they got here so she couldn't relax and let down. Laura had her lie down on her bed, and after I'd made hot compresses from the good hand towels and made the woman a glass of choco-late milk, Laura repaired her with the milk and the wet heat.

The young woman said, It won't ever

be any better than this. Then she sighed so long and hard, the wind fluttered the baby's hair, and she held her to her chest. Laura paid her for work the two of us did and paid her not to come back and do more. After the girl had been on the payroll a few weeks, she had to move with the man who'd upset her, but she sent Laura a thimble made by Starletta's mother, which is how I remember her, when I hear her sigh when Laura sews.

Laura set out leftovers and took a plate to her room, telling me she'd feel better in a while and come out for the show, and if I wanted to make a pallet on the sofa, since we'd be up late, that was fine. She'd seen the note and was glad for the reminder. I gave her a handful of things I'd torn out of the magazines, telling her one of them was about women writing love letters to Charles Manson. She smiled and said their mothers must be proud, and then she set her plate on the table and told me, You know another thing about this house? There hasn't been a man here, not to stay, since my father left it, and that has to account for how bad it feels when there's a struggle, there's been nothing to accustom the place to fear.

I said, I don't want you to think I'm afraid you'd let me get hurt.

She said, And you know that.

When I said, Absolutely, she said, Okay then, move over. Phyllis Diller's on a special this evening. Did you know?

I hadn't known it, but when we located the program we began laughing and decided to be irresponsible and let the room go, and when the late comedy show came on, she said she couldn't listen to me anymore until she'd gotten down the thesaurus and found synonyms for amazing. We talked about a million people with the popularity boxes voting the show off and said we'd burn for being conceited and then came down a peg when we didn't know who Buck Henry was despite how he no doubt couldn't walk roads elsewhere without being mobbed. But, I told her, I know enough. I know why you want to close the door to what happened. We've had October in this house.

Nine

On Sunday, we drove to the verge of the mountain part of the state, where potters hold open houses and invite people in to observe them at the wheel and ask questions. We walked around, bought some of their wares, and had supper at a Shoney's. Tired, we got home after dark to find Stuart's bicycle leaned against the front steps and him sitting there waiting, squinting at us in the dim porch light, with a paper sack in his hands. Laura said to pray for a second wind to blow through, and then we took our new vases out of the car, pulled his bicycle out of the damp, and invited him in.

Watching him slope to my room, Laura said, Just pay some attention to him, and make sure there's nothing alive in the sack.

He'd been crying. He told me nothing was the matter, he only needed to talk to me privately before he died. He closed my door and laid his coat across the foot of my bed, and then he flopped back on it and looked at the ceiling, asking, Would you mind? Huh, I swear before God, I wish you wouldn't. If you do, you'll need to allow me to stay here until I get up.

In case he rolled over, I sat against my pillows and asked if the reason he'd been crying had to do with the sack, which was moving up and down on his stomach. The sack, he said, came after Mama hit me like a man. She said it was coming and dared me to run. I should of left before she did it, but later on, I told her I had to go see a man about a dog, and then I rode on up here. You didn't say you'd be gone.

So you waited how long? I asked him.

I hadn't needed to ask about the dog because people say it when they don't want you to know where they're going, usually to get a present for you. He'd slept off and on outside the house, he wasn't sure how long without a clock, but he said he'd definitely been out there from can see to can't see.

When I asked how things turned out with the dog, he said, I got it, but I need to tell you first I hauled heaving outside your house. The rain they said was coming tomorrow, should take care of it so you don't have to stand elsewhere and wait on the bus, but, huh, I think I broke some ribs, and my lips dried. Does it look like I'm going to get a blood blister?

I said, You could use some Vaseline,

but please fold your lip back up before I have to remember Luther's attractive cousin.

He couldn't listen for feeling over his skin and mashing around to make sure, he said, his mother hadn't injured him beyond whiplash when his head spun around.

I said, Stuart, your mother, I know, has a hard time when she gets to the end of her rope, like yesterday, when she rolled you out of the car. Do you need Laura to try and find your father at one of those places he stays at on the highway?

No, he said, she wasn't trying to kill me yesterday. She was running late to be early in line for a store closing holding a special. She dislikes for you to move slow. One reason she likes you is you go in high gear.

Laura had once called him a nitwit with a heart of gold who would wander the earth unless someone was there to corral him, so when it appeared he'd come to the end of his explanation and locked a gaze on the ceiling with tears shivering over his eyes, I said, Climb up around here by me, Stuart, and let's end the suspense on the sack. I think I need to be complimented for not snatching it.

Yes, he said, you're a patient girl. Knocking against the headboard and shoving a pillow roll behind his neck, he said, The pain may be from squeezing the handlebars with my mother on my mind.

Tell it, I said, I've had the same sensations going on lately about my aunt.

Bingo, he said, on what's in the sack, but before I let you have it, I need to say I wish I'd allowed you to behave your way at the fair. I'm sorry about that now on account of the trouble it caused from what happened when Laura phoned up my mother this morning, early, so it wouldn't eat at her with the two of you out trying to have fun.

When he stalled again and I told him to start with the first memory and work his way through, he said, Huh, okay, so I was in the hall, and my mother, she picked up the phone. I wasn't going to listen until I could tell it was Laura and heard Mama say, It's not a problem for me to tell you what I know. Nadine tells me things like I want to hear them, and if I'd thought it was my business, I would've gotten in touch with you immediately. Nadine knows how I feel about her treating a child like a cur dog, but she feels bound and compelled to talk to me like I've ignored it.

What, I said, was the topic, you know, the theme?

He said, One was Mama telling Laura she would've taken you in to raise if she'd felt straighter after she had Henry and believed she could manage the two she already had, which was a shock to me, and a letdown, knowing you could've been a sister. The other main thing said was your aunt has been running things for your grandmother since she died, and she isn't leaving because of Dora. Dora's the excuse for her mother to be gone when people find out she's been collecting rent from the family that rents your old house that everybody knows you need for school and how you despise taking from Laura. People know that. When they comment on you working like a grown woman, I tell them you go and do on your own and plan to.

I thought the bank owned the house. I thought the man at the bank took over everything that belonged to my grandmother, and she'd left my aunt a chunk to raise Dora on. She's been in private school. I passed by the shoe store last year and saw her in there trying on leather boots. Is there anything else? Did it sound like it'd be enough to get from now through college and medical school on? Do you mean to say I own the house?

Yes, he said, and I don't know how much she's tooken from you. The last thing I heard was a whoosh from Mama swinging back, but I think she was upset more because she likes to believe Laura thinks highly of her, like they have the same standing, and me telling you got her caught carrying a story. She'd already phoned up several individuals on it though she told Laura she might've mentioned it to one.

I said, I hope it helps to see the reason she hurt you. It's smart of you to know.

Handing me the sack, he said, Smart was taking the Phillips head when I took the other one and left.

Inside the sack was a doorknob I recognized. We had a glass one like this. Did you take it off my old house for me?

Yes, he said, smiling, and I know you're going to ask me why. I planned on saying, huh, to make you ask me questions.

Okay, I said, so if that didn't satisfy me, what did you plan to say next?

He reached over and turned the doorknob a touch and said, It was on the outside, and you've wanted something from there for a long time is the main reason. Then hearing how everything's stirred up again with your aunt, I said to myself, Ellen needs me to give her the doorknob so she can shut all the rooms and close her old house. Don't take it the wrong way, but you live in it so much of the time is what I see. The doorknob is for you to use in your mind, so don't take it over there and try to install it back on because, huh, you have no idea how disappointed your mother would be if she knew how the family kept her house looking inside. They're very common people, Ellen, and your mother was so tall and clean. Keep looking up when you ride by. I'll let everybody know to keep helping you.

I'd made myself not look at the house by making sure someone was always riding beside me if I had to be that far across the river. Martha or Luther, for instance, always told me to quickly notice an odd cloud in the sky, and Stuart liked to say he saw rockets launched from Cape Canaveral. When I asked if the house was completely decrepit, he said, About, and I couldn't bring a dead potter plant or string and strowed trash from the yard. Remember when your mother ran out of air blowing up the pool for us to play in?

No, I said, it's one of the things that slipped through and now I'm not able.

Don't worry about it, he told me. I've got it for you. You see, where I remember Miss Shine doubling over, falling, and you down there with her, giving her breath, and me running across the road for Starletta's father to come is where these shiftless individuals have a smoking pile of trash, not something you'd make a living off of, Ellen, but like, when they weren't home, I figured they'd gone to get more garbage to throw on it. No family of four can create that much trash.

I didn't know how I understood what to do when my mother fell. Maybe she fainted so often that I'd looked up directions. I didn't know, and no scenes came back, but when I was beginning to feel too sunken in from too much lost, he said, But Ellen, let me tell you what the good thing was. Let me tell you how it was the same weather in the yard from where the wind used to pick up the pecan leaves and cyclone them. The only thing missing when I saw the leaves twirl a circle was you and me watching Starletta squatted down, reaching out to pat it and her having the blues when it stopped, not meaning to say it was a ghost there on account of I remember the ground there had a habit of cyclones coming on. But remember another thing?

I probably don't, I said, and thank you for these, but they're sufficient. You can get supersaturated. I don't know if your class got to that, I mean I can't use anymore until these absorb.

I ran a experiment on it, he said, with Luther and a glass of water and some sand from the park in town.

When I asked how things had turned out, as he got up and lay the doorknob on my dresser and came back for us to watch it like a display on view, he said, Polished dirt wasn't worth a damn, and since it was a take-home test where the answer was the fastest rate, we dug loam and used it. We'd used town sand to keep from turning in mud, but it wasn't the answer, just a waste of gas, tires, and oil to go get it.

You learn, I said. Then he let me turn on the side with my back to him, and he let us be quiet until he began going through his coat pockets and suggested I sit up and look at the foot of my bed if I wanted the surprise of my life.

Before I did it, I asked if he realized it was Sunday night and he usually had pajamas on by now, and he said he did, but he was wearing something better. He had his paisley necktie on. He pulled a leg up under him and leaned toward me and said, I meant the doorknob, so don't believe I didn't, and now I need you to trust me on a instadecision I made when Mama took and hit me.

I expected him to say he wanted to start technical school at Harvard, and Henry was dragging his suitcase up the road right now for him to stay with Laura and me in the meantime, but he said, I may not have a ring for your finger. Like said, it was a instadecision, so it wasn't time to go speak to Sears about the extent of me credick.

Did she slap you, I said, in the face or the head? Sears, extend you credit? Do you hear yourself?

I do, he said, and, huh, that's exactly what you're going to be saying to me next Saturday.

On Candid Camera, I told him. Are you going to tell me now or later I'm expecting.

Cart before the horse, he said. I just wanted to tell you I apologize your finger has to stay empty for a while, but allow it to make you feel better to know the man has a very clean truck.

When I asked what truck, he said, The truck the man drives tires in. He has told me I could ride and bring a friend anytime, anyplace, anywhere, so when he comes tomorrow, I'll make arrangements and be sure he knows not to pile anything in the seat next Saturday or ask his own wife to travel with him. It's our day, and, huh, I swear before God, I'm not likely to share it.

Stuart, I said, hold on. We don't have a day.

That's why, he said, I think Saturday's good. We'd spend the night at the South of the Border with the Valentime bed and one that pulls out the wall, which I'd appreciate having because I wonder what it'd be like to sleep on one. Then he'd carry us back here on Sunday. Harvey and Luther said they'd give us a list of what fireworks they wanted.

You told them about this?

He said, I rode by their houses a minute before I knew you weren't home, but don't take it the wrong way. I just

said I was going across the state lines
with you. I didn't say why, and they said
they'd appreciate us bringing them back
firecrackers is all. You know you can't
beat Pedro's variety, and Ellen, you don't
need to worry about me being one of
these that run out and play cards and set
off explosives with their friends and
leave you alone of an evening.

When I said that wasn't what I'd been
thinking at all, he said, I know, I was off
on a tange. What I was saying was I'll
tell the man to make sure everything's in
order and see if he can get the South of
the Border church and the motel and lay
it to his charge-a-plate if I can't get my
mother to sign for me to draw out of the
bank this week. She'll sign for a married
son though, and I've got fair money to
last until then, so, huh, I'd say we're in
the right shape, particular since you
didn't know how high my bank figure is
since a certain grandfather died.

Mother of God, Stuart, I said, did
you just wink?

And you'll be getting used to it soon, he said, lesser nerves, lesser mistakes, more of me being the one in the lead.

He more or less fell forward and got me around the waist, so there wasn't a choice but to be there to hear, Oh God, I'm dying to cross the state line with you.

He wouldn't let go when we heard his mother slamming through the door. A man, he said, would tell her he's a man. He'd care for his woman and fix tricky situations.

Stuart, I said, your mother is going to box you. Laura's going to be confused. I appreciate the doorknob, but we'll talk about the other at school.

Sitting up and pulling his arm away, he interrupted me, saying, Which I forgot to say I want you to keep attending.

Trying to erase the picture of Jerry Lee Lewis and his child bride from my mind, I said, I don't think it's legal anywhere, and you know you don't want me to be an outlaw.

I know, he said, and you know the family that eats off records? The mother changed four birth certifs so they'd take her children in school sooner. One of them sits next to me and looks, huh, seven. How hard could it be? Do you have your certif or did it get tooken from your old house? I could get started this evening.

He didn't care that Laura could be heard calming his mother down in the kitchen. She's not the woman I want running me, he said. And you don't know how I'd take and look after you. You know the colored man who works for Daddy and lives in the little blue house with the roof you said looked like they painted it with chocolate milk? Well, he moved out, so we could move in.

So, I said, I just stay home from college?

He said, They've got one here, and it'd be fine for you to go and be in the house of an evening for me to ask how

soon supper is and what you learned
and so forth. I mean, huh, it's modern.
I mean, I don't picture you at the ironing board, but it's not my fault what I
see. That's just the way it is, Ellen. But
it's fine on the county college. I wouldn't
bother you out of school any more than
you'd stop me from opening service bo-
nanza locations up and down the inner-
state highway. It won't be the women's
lib moving either though. You deserve
to live like the lady with the government
husband they had on trial that summer
when you said you admired how she
stayed fixed and said her legs stayed
crossed to where she'd hit the floor
twisted if she went to stand up.

I said, We're not John and Maureen
Dean.

Which reminds me to tell you, he
said, glasses run in my family, so I'll be
headed to the optimist probably here directly, and I'll see if he carries some like
the man had on. Then I'll come in the
door for you to say they become me. It'd

make you feel more like you'd gone on and gone to Harvard. And long as I'm on the topic, ask yourself if Harvard was the one who showed up here and got you.

Giving me time to settle that for myself, he stared off to listen and gauge how much time we had before Laura had done the most she could do with his mother. I told him quietly, Stuart, I didn't try out for the Harvard football team. This isn't like the time the coach came out here and slept on the couch at Luther's and bought groceries and outfits for everybody, luring his brother to play on his team.

He wasn't listening. He turned to me and said, What I want, for the largest part, is to have a little blue home with you, Ellen. I was outside it this afternoon, and all I could think is how pretty you'd look in the yard with clean tennis shoes on, sweeping a rake. When you're through, I want to watch you drink a glass of chocolate milk, and then I want to fry a steak and watch you eat it. You used to look odd, but I swear before God, you've gotten very, very good-looking, at least to me. And now, it sounds like my mother's going to be in here any minute, but don't say anything. She doesn't know, but, huh, I'll tell her.

I said, So she finds you missing and hears all this. I'll leave the two of you alone.

I wish you wouldn't, he said. It'll come out better with you here. The closest I came to talking to her about anything on this order was when she talked to me about women one time and said I should try for the quiet ones and leave the ones more like you alone on account of you have to be tough to keep a smart woman from dating out on you.

Everything else he'd been talking about left my mind, and all I could think was how his mother had gotten this warped impression of me. I almost wanted her to hurry so I could ask how she could believe that enough to say it like a fact. I said, She's known me all my life. She should be thinking the opposite. What have I done to make her think that?

Listen, listen, he said, I know you aren't that way. I mean, I wouldn't have to worry about you dating out on me, would I?

No, I told him, of course not, no. You know I'm not the kind of person who'd date out on their husband.

His mother knocked on the door as she opened it and looked hard at both of us. Laura was looking over her shoulder. I was about to ask what I'd said or done to make her think I'd deliberately hurt her son or anyone else, when Stuart shouted, Come on in! It's no time like now to meet my bride-to-be, Ellen Foster! Come on in, ladies! Congratulate me and my honey.

Ten

STUART CALLED AT MIDNIGHT, CRY-ing. He claimed that his mother put on a false front in my room and then took it off on the way home and tried to beat him to death with it. He said she'd backhanded him, put out his hearing, and caused him to bleed from the ears, and when I asked whether she'd kept the car in the road, he said, You've heard her say how strong she is from carrying groceries in the house by herself? Well, she is. She's strong armed in both arms and got fairly good aim.

His mother actually had a reputation for being able to drive with one hand and change a diaper with the other one. She was also often called Job, Laura said after they left, for extremely sensible reasons. That could now include being asked repeatedly on her way out with Stuart whether she felt rooked out of planning a grand wedding, whether she'd carry him by the banker's house to get his inheritance, as tomorrow felt all over like too long to wait, and whether she'd accept the honor of our firstborn being named after her. He said, I feel a female coming on, O Mama!

Laura said, Barring killing him and standing over him lying there in his green sweater and prison shoes to give him the worst blow of all, how do you intend to break through this world he's in with the news?

That I'm not marrying him now or ever? I asked.

She said, More than one thing at a time is a thousand times too much for someone that fragile to bear.

One of his themes, I told her, has always been apologizing for something he tried to believe because of pressure from his mother. With anybody else, it'd be an individual versus society conflict, though she tends to come at you with the force of a large group.

So, you think he's going to take it all back?

Yes, I said, and soon. I'll tell him it's okay, but that'll take a while, and I'm tired, so when the phone rings, I may have to not hear it until I get the next wind.

Then lie here with me and listen to something I've had to wait for the next wind to say as well. You need to know, Ellen, I wasn't trying to hide anything from you about your aunt and the house. It didn't feel right to pass along secondhand information that could be contradicted by fact. I was planning to talk to an attorney and your aunt and then come to you when I had things straight. I hope that can be okay. I was looking after your interests, but I'm afraid it feels like I'm making the way to do it up as I go along.

I trusted her, and I told her, You're the one to see what's happening for me. I see it, and it's fine. But what do I do if I own my old house? What if Stuart had it right?

She said we'd decide when she sorted out the truth. After we talked about the state line, the tire truck and fireworks, the ironing board and the blue house, and I was finally in bed, Stuart called. It wasn't in his mother's nature to go at him that severely, but it was in his recent mental makeup to take the phone with the long cord to bed with him and call me saying he'd been direly injured. Love or lust was new to his personality. Four years ago, if you'd have asked him what he wanted, he would've said a new cat and a rainproof tent, and now it was like he had no choice but to let me in on how the torment was tightening the grip.

Blowing his nose, I pictured in the pillowcase, he said, I wanted you to know I won't be in school tomorrow, too shamed, and mad, too, about how you got tooken by your family. I know your aunt's going to bring your mother's things to you, and I know she's got to get straight with you on the owed rent, but I'd appreciate you not mentioning I took the doorknob off the house though I ought to be apologizing to you. I'll put it back on for you this week.

What you did doesn't qualify for cringing, I told him. I'll see you in the morning.

It felt like only an hour passed before I was on the bus in front of Stuart's house, watching Henry get on holding a biscuit. He sat across the aisle from me, splitting it open on top of his spelling book. I asked where his brother was and he said, Fighting with Mama over you in the kitchen. He said his eyes swoll too bad for school. She said, huh, he'd be swoll shut next time he goes up yonder to Ellen Foster's house to be the fool and be crazy.

Henry, I said, what are they saying about me exactly?

I had to wait for him to distribute a packet of grape jelly he'd taken from a massive glass jar of restaurant condiments his father empties his pockets into after a trip the way people do with their change. Chewing, he said, She said leave you loam. Said you got it made. Stuart said you don't. She said he knows half it and to shut up and put a bag of froze peas on his eyes. Tole him he knows where they are afore she chunked the bag at him, huh.

By the time we unloaded at the main doors, I'd poked Henry from every direction, hoping I'd hit something concrete he'd stored up about what Stuart knowing half of things meant, but I learned nothing outside of what height of desperation it takes to ignore your friends rubbernecking you block a sticky-faced third grader from his classroom to urge him to say why, from his point of view, would his mother be saying I had it made.

Martha was at her locker and overheard me asking him whether his mother might've said I had it made because I might go to Harvard, trying to see what rang bells. She said, Ellen, he came in the store Saturday and shoplifted the cake mix he lives on again. He's Henry. Turn him loose.

I told him to go on and then I helped Martha stand there and stare in her locker like you do with the refrigerator door open. The problem was the stacked and crammed boxes of women's monthly supplies in every variety from teen styles to things Luther saw and said his uncle used on horses in heat that she kept on hand for Mrs. Delacroix and lunchroom ladies Nature hadn't left yet. When I asked if she needed to use some room in mine, she said, I don't know. I can't think.

I said, Then did you hear anything in the store about me having it made this weekend?

No, she said, nothing. All that happened this weekend was Daddy ran across a deal on a car he said I could have if I helped pay for it. Unless you have it made to where you want to buy five hundred dollars worth of Kotex, I don't want to hear about it.

So you didn't hear either, I asked her, about me owning my old house and it not belonging to the bank, nothing about my aunt taking the money off from it?

She said, No, but that's good news. You can evict the trash that lives in it if for no other reason than they haven't paid their bill in a year and have the gall to send a toddler in there to charge groceries. I hope they've been paying rent. How are you going to get it out of your aunt?

I explained how Laura was going to call a lawyer that morning and see where things stood, but I said, I wouldn't be surprised if I was owed somewhere in the thousands, which is why my aunt's leaving for Texas but telling people it's because my cousin's pregnant.

Walking outside to the low stone wall, she said, That doesn't sound right. She did much worse to you before and stayed here with everybody knowing it.

It hadn't occurred to me, but she was right. I told her Laura would have everything outlined by the time I got home. I felt looser in the neck than usual, knowing something would be made right. Some people already on the wall told Martha and me to look across the road at where they were watching four boys in the high school parking lot while they sat on a tailgate and cleaned shotguns and then sent the skinny one off with two buckets for ice from the lunchroom. They dumped those into a large chest before they unzipped out of their camouflage covers and got their books together to attend classes until it was time to take what they'd shot home and please their mothers with how fresh everything still is. Watching them and listening for our names to call back present, a girl named Mae who rarely talks but to herself, said, I bet that's us next year.

I was stupefied. Then she said, Hey Ellen, my mother was on the same train with you far as Washington. You didn't see her, but I was thinking, if you go on to Harvard, what're you going to do about school?

I said I hated I'd missed her mother and waited for a way to defend myself for dropping out of school, but Luther jumped the wall from behind me and sat, looking down at her. Do you think she belongs here, period? He said, It's not like the truant officer's going to go drag her back from Harvard. How many classes have you seen her in? She's been in the library, already good as gone, and rules don't apply to high-IQ people. She could get the thing the Pope gave the lady in the paper if they took and forced her across the road.

A papal dispensation, I told him, but I don't think it'd get that far, especially with me not being Catholic and not going to church for three years.

Martha said, I think those are for if you get knocked up.

Everybody knew and seemed to tell me at once, Maybe your cousin could get one.

So I asked whether anyone had heard anything about me having it made, and Harvey said, Stuart's mother called mine and said it. After a few others said his mother had phoned up theirs with the same news, I said, All I know is my old house belongs to me, but it doesn't rate the easy life, I don't think.

Luther said, You should fix it up for Marvin to stay in before his house slides off in the river.

I said I didn't know what to do yet, but it was being taken care of, and I'd ask Stuart directly if the thought of it didn't wear me out. People said, Tell it! Who knows where he is?

At home in the kitchen, I said, too downtrodden to be here.

Harvey said, He came to my house wild yesterday afternoon, and when he said he was going to leave for Luther's and over the pasture to your house, I said I'd better ride with him to make sure they wouldn't have to drag the river with the wide net later that evening. He said he'd bring firecrackers from Pedro's, but you don't know what to believe.

Believe, I said, the only explosions on this road are going to be from Laura going up against my aunt. Stuart had a plan to cross the state line for a strange purpose, but, for mercy, it didn't work out.

Good God, Martha said. Girls who didn't get the Pope excusing the baby, or whatever he does, go for quickie weddings down there. If you're not on the way to Florida or out of explosives, it's why you'd go. I'd imagine Stuart's a bad enough wreck that you'd need to go to Harvard sheerly to escape the hounding on account of he's going to keep coming. Sorry to say it, but the only person I can see you setting up housekeeping with is Stuart or the one from the book you made us all read, the screwup with the gray hair.

Holden Caulfield, I told her. This is depressing.

But Ellen, Mae said, don't places like Harvard want you to have a sport or a talent or something to make you more well-rounded? Don't take it the wrong way, but anybody can ride a bicycle.

Luther said, Mae, when's the last time you filled out the crossword puzzle or read something outside Guideposts?

I said, I put a letter in with the scores and some themes, saying I hadn't had time to develop a talent. If they call for a sport, you're right, there's the bicycle.

And Ellen, Marvin said, has always had good posture, but Ellen, hey, you think you might allow Daddy and me to rent your house?

I told him I'd have to see what was what, thinking he must be extremely concerned about drowning asleep to want to move into a house that two people had died in and where everybody knew I didn't as much live with my father as hide from him. Despite how the family of four had treated it like a routine rural house to trash, I often wondered if they heard pleading in the walls, great sad sounds you associate with locations in the universe where good and evil and peace and desperation clash.

Mae had been mumbling at the other end of the wall, and when I heard Luther shout out loud, She is too good, and she has to think it, but when's the last time you heard her reminding somebody of it? Do you see her cut out to care what's up with Lottie Moon Society or going out for the softball team? When's the last time you went somewhere to know about how you get to go?

Nowhere yet, she said, but we're going to Colonial Williamsburg for Thanksgiving.

I told Luther not to bother, I was fine, but everybody stopped and tuned in the way they do when somebody says they're going somewhere besides White Lake. Mae said, It's my parents' anniversary, and when my father asked what my mother wanted, she said she wanted to go to Williamsburg and stay where you're not allowed to cook, so he parted the flock early.

I said, You're taking a vacation on chickens?

I wouldn't go to Williamsburg, Marvin said, ducking his head to his shoulder like a horrible memory was coming back. Have you heard how easy it is to fall in a soap vat?

Martha said, When Ellen and me went to Tweetsie Railroad last year, the Indians robbed the train in tennis shoes.

After I added on how there was nothing in the gift store there you wanted,

Harvey said, We went to pick my uncle up at the airport once, and you could live on what they carry in the vending machine area if you were out in the woods for a year.

Marvin said, You'd lack a place to plug them in.

But listen, Harvey said, to what happened to this man the time his wife plugged the wringer washing machine in behind his back, jerked his arm through, and mashed him to where his neck went into his head.

What I heard, Luther said, as the teacher leaned out the window and shouted the roll, was the woman mashed the man's peter.

We gathered our belongings to go inside, laughing but squinting, trying to see if the story could be real, how and why the man would've been angled up on the washing machine, except Mae, who had to let us know before we opened the wide main hall doors, My mother's got different tours planned. She wouldn't allow me around a soap vat.

Mine either, I told her. It's a story is all.

Mae, Martha said, can you please turn back into Helen Keller and stop reminding me how if Ellen does leave here, there's nobody to stop a plague of ignorance from taking over?

I didn't have to separate into the library that morning because an assembly was scheduled for the county health nurse to show a personal hygiene film. If I wasn't off to myself, I didn't want to feel both near and far but home, so I said, I need to leave the ill will on the low wall. Being the one they said has it made ought to give me the right to say I'm on the verge of a big sweep of things that's more than likely going to clean away anybody who doesn't wish me well.

Mae said, It sounds selfish. You just want people around that wish you well all the time.

Before I could explain how I hadn't meant I wanted to be with people who told me only what I wanted to hear and how a thoughtless family was back and weighing down on me, Stuart's large arm was over my head, holding the heavy gym door open. Ignoring questions about why he was sore-eyed, I imagined from an ointment he'd applied to hurry the frozen peas, he shouted over the noise inside, What's the topic? Ellen getting to have people that wish her well with her all the time? I think it's a good idea, but I'll be able to say more on it later, when I'm less partway blinded.

When we were seated on the bleachers, when the lights went down and Luther whispered with a kind of blowing, damp heat into my hair, Hey, hey, I just thought of the way to train the wild out of the bobcat faster. Treat him like he's already a cat, and he'll get some habits that can sink into him later.

Thinking you could do worse than having Luther wishing you nothing but well, I said, And then, Wa-La, he'll be a pet?

Exactly, he said, behave to him the way you expect him to behave.

I told him it was a revelation, and then we were all told to hush, but knowing we had a few minutes before the health nurse repeated it, Martha spoke over my shoulder, saying, Listen, you've got a head for business. You know how shamed boys are to buy their things? They stalk around the store and wait for one of my brothers to wait on them, and on Saturday nights, town boys come in droves to be incognito, so think and tell me if it makes sense for me to branch out from female supplies to male and get somebody honest like Stuart to sell them next year.

Thinking this wasn't a model conversation for Dr. Bok to know about, unless Martha was about to tell me her idea had its beginnings in Thebes, I said, His brother's sharper, but they've all got another year to get less goofy, so you'd find somebody willing to split a profit hand over fist with you. Isn't it taking money the store could be making?

She said, What I'd make, I wouldn't have to beg for. They still pay me what I find sweeping, but hold the fort and notice it's dark and Starletta's not in your lap.

I had to tell her Starletta's class had been banned because of the sexy subject matter involved with a venereal disease movie. You wouldn't think new state politics would've had the trickle-down effect on us after less than a year of extremely strict people in office, but they'd made certain decisions on church and state and free speech that I didn't mention to Harvard. With of all the things off in my background, saying the library was sent a list of books to remove, which Mrs. Delacroix and I ignored with anxiety, made it sound like the atmosphere was too tinged with danger. Although if you'd seen the books they wanted out, it would've felt like you were tied down and made to hear hostage takers shout warped ideas and lies.

Starletta would've loved to see the husband of the witch in Bewitched playing the captain of a high school basketball team who wrestles with venereal disease. He and his girlfriend are perfectly popular, riding around with the gang crammed into a kind of jalopy automobile, but they don't expose how social he was on a trip to the city before the movie started until he's in the locker room, in despair and pulling his best friend aside to tell him, I've got a problem, down there. They glance down at the front of his uniform shorts, and now they're both looking destroyed in the face but determined to make it through and not risk college or his girl finding out. They decide to involve a hood who's more in the know and says he should get to a doctor on the double.

Then the boy's instantly sitting on an examining table, rolling his sleeve down and thanking the doctor for the shot he just gave him, and then they turn to face you and warn against trading your family, friends, and future for one night of what they both admit sounds like a barrel of fun. A nurse wheels in a blackboard with some statistics listed on it, and after the doctor runs through them, he says if numbers bore you, then the weak-kneed beware and everybody get a load of these close-ups of sores and let them convince you. The boy chimes in then, holding a basketball out of nowhere, to say, summarized, And remember, your teen years are like, say, practice for the biggest game of your life. Sure, make the scene dating, and get to know all types of people, but take it from someone who's been there, abstinence always makes the heart grow fonder.

The music comes on, and he's playing basketball again and smiling at his buddy like he's glad all that's over with and winking at his girl, who's screaming her head off for him, clueless she's soon to be coated in sores down there or gossiped about as the news of how untrue he was to her begins leaking out. You could tell it's all going to end up swell for her because it always does. Then, just after I told Martha too bad she couldn't sell hot date supplies at the movie high school, Starletta's teacher ran through the door and to the podium, disrupting the nurse's wrap-up to tell Ellen Foster to come down to go with her to the main hall immediately. Addled, she said it wasn't a general emergency, just Ellen's, and then she ran back to the door and waited for me.

I moved without asking why. The faster you go, the more likely they are to be alive. You don't need experience in getting there miraculously in time if you have new endings ready for everything you weren't able to run to before and so well-nursed and strengthened by the time they've spent in your heart that your movements can be swift and easy, recited like the gifts instinct offers at night, giving mendicant, palmer, pilgrim, prior, tricking and stopping, sleepy and proud, cried in goose, alas.

When I turned a corner onto the wide hall, I saw people edged around the outskirts of a cyclone, yelling to egg Starletta on or to stop. Breaking in was like sticking an arm in a fan, and the adults who'd decided to wait on me to try it stepped aside and watched because they needed to send good will my way and flatter me into breaking up the brawl so Starletta's mother wouldn't have too many injured places to count and hold their noses to when Starletta got home. While they were shouting ways for me to stay safe and dodge flailing blows, I pushed through to the center and saw her arched in a flying leap onto a gigantic white boy's back. She held on and beat him with one hand, and then she'd clamp her legs and go at his head with both. When I found a way to get my hands to pull her off him, she was blowing like a horse and soaked from the milk from all the cartons scattered across the floor.

The boy was new but familiar to me because he'd frightened her before and caused her mother to come to school repeatedly, saying either they make him leave Starletta alone or she'd have to leave until they could tell her he'd been enrolled elsewhere. He'd loped out of the classroom behind her when she left to collect milk money from the grammar grade rooms and then waited for her to come out of the lunchroom, pushing a metal cart loaded with cartons. He knew her routine, how she stopped between rooms to handle the pumpkin pin and how she'd grip the bar and put her weight against it to keep it from drifting, overall getting the largest possible bang you could get out of a morning. When the boy couldn't take his craving for milk or beauty anymore, he'd lurched out to rob her the same way he had before. This time, she wouldn't turn loose of the cart, and so his last good time for a while was drinking the fourteenth container of milk she let him have in peace.

I carried her to the library and let her down onto the large satin pillows she's always luxuriating on in the Easy Reader section, blissful, but when I covered her with the sweater Mrs. Delacroix handed me, she turned on her side and stiffened with her hands pressed between her knees and her eyes closed. You could hear the commotion of the boy in the office, and Mrs. Delacroix said, Go to my desk and call her mother. I'll watch her. Hulking sonabitch, grain-fed fool.

Her mother wanted to know the details on the phone so she could begin sorting them on the way there and not appear, swinging. When she arrived, she was quiet but ruthless in a way she didn't care whether colored women had free permission to behave or not. After she was in the office a minute, she changed Starletta into a dry dress she'd come in holding and said, Go get her things. I'm stopping by Laura's for her to help me think, so come if you want to go home, but don't stop to linger.

Starletta's classmates scattered like shot pool balls after the brawl, so I was able to scrape out her toy- and candy-jammed cubby into my book satchel in peace and then rush to the library, where Mrs. Delacroix said Starletta's mother had been in a white woman hurry to leave and motioned to where they were waiting in the car. I flopped in beside Starletta, who lay her head in my lap while her mother drove, kneading her legs.

I said, How did you do it? If I'd been in your shoes, I would've gone blank and let him sit on the cart and offered him straws. To answer, she pulled up her dress to show me the two pairs of underwear that she wore on mornings when her mother showed her the calendar to remind her of milk days and other times when she knew the extra sensation of being held securely would help her stay brave.

Eleven

THE UNKNOWN CAR IN THE YARD didn't grab my attention as much as Laura flying out of the house like we were the rescue squad there to save her. Slowing down as she came toward us, she was wild-eyed and staggering on the heels she disliked wearing on the thick gravel. As we got out of the car, I said, You look like Ava again, after she's been with her house boyfriends in the ocean. Are you trying to keep us from seeing the Spaniard who owns this car? I was wondering if this is what you did with the day while I was in school.

She said, No, your aunt, your cousin, your lawyer sent them over.

When Starletta wrapped herself around her mother's chest with the same stubborn grip she'd held on the boy, I said, She either senses what's in the house or remembers, and that's fair warning for me to get my bicycle out and ride her to the store. I know I said I wanted to talk to them, but she's in the flesh now, here.

Starletta's mother told Laura, I don't know if you notice it isn't time for school to turn out yet.

Laura looked down at the business-looking pumps she would've worn to a lawyer's office and asked herself why she'd worn them on sharp rocks. Then she said, To tell the truth, I wondered a second, and my mind turned it back, absolutely out of room after a world of information this morning and then these two inside. What's wrong? Star-letta looks unstrung.

Starletta's mother said, I offered to bring Ellen home after she took Starletta away from a mess, but it can save for us to go on into this one.

Walking inside, I didn't see a box or bag in the living room, but Laura nod-ded and motioned to say my mother's belongings were outside in my aunt's car. It was fishy that it hadn't come in with them, so before they could stand up to greet me, I had to ask whether they'd left their car locked.

Aunt Nadine was still tight fat, like there was a hidden place on her where skin was stretched together and safety pinned, and I knew her tone would say I was still abnormal, but it didn't matter. She shimmied to the edge of the sofa and screamed, Well ho! Look who's here and not any more able to wait a minute, but you wouldn't think it, not with how grown you've grown, and in the paper all the time with the prizes and so forth and so on, like somebody else.

She meant it as a compare and contrast of the present me to the disaster ingrate she'd told to leave her life, with Dora agreeing, rabid to get rid of me and rip through the remainder of her many Christmas presents. There hadn't been much more room for Dora to continue into on the growth chart, but the baby on the way drove her over the highest percentiles. I said, Hey Dora, I'd like to run out there and get the box so you don't have to worry about accidentally taking it.

Dora said, I won't. I'm the one that packed Aunt Shine's things for you.

I sat by Laura on the ottoman she'd rolled in front of the fireplace, and as Starletta's mother came back in from settling Starletta to play in my room, I realized how Dora was the only person I didn't become highly jealous of when I heard her say my mother's name. So few people who said her name like they knew her deserved to, and when Dora said it again, I didn't hear myself shouting inside like a hateful toddler, Mine.

Dora said, I put so much in, I thought I better not try to come up these steps with it, but I'm glad to go with you to carry it.

And you know how my back is, my aunt said, nodding at me like her pet bodily complaint had been on my front burner.

I whispered to Laura, We're getting the hustle.

Laura said, And you couldn't begin to know. The box can't compare to what I need to talk to you about.

But Ellen needs to look at Dora first, my aunt said, and tell me if she doesn't look like something.

Laura said, She looks very nice, about to pop. I'm going to get the papers we're here to talk about and be right back.

Dora was mortified, and Starletta's mother and I were mortified for her, so critically that the least painful thing I could find to ask her was, Where did you find your bracelets?

Still looking down from when her mother had spoken, Dora said, I was about to ask you that about your top, but they come from somewhere in town I forgot.

We got them, her mother said, when we got the news and decided to spruce up because of how hard it is to stay girlie the heavier you get.

Starletta's mother got up, abandoning me to check on how quiet things were in my bedroom. She had to go back there and stand stunned that a woman who used an awful silliness to make her coarseness pleasing could've been related to my mother. I'd always believed my aunt genuinely loved her sister, but now you sensed somebody who wasn't graceful or smart, scratching to keep up with the older one who was. I saw it in how unsteady she was, how out of place she looked in our house. I wasn't as afraid of her, on my ground, in a room that Laura made, and with Laura coming back in now, with more of my mother's favor than I'd seen.

Sitting by me with a folder on her knees, Laura said, And you've considered flying to Texas, I'd think. It's a long way of open opportunity to be stranded, this far along.

When my aunt said the doctor outlawed flying, Dora said, What he said was don't go at all.

I'd never seen anything as dejecting as my cousin's permanent wave, which, she said, kinked on account of the hair chemicals either don't take or overtake when they mix with the pregnancy chemicals.

She kept looking down and peeking up, like she was checking to make sure we weren't glued to the other ways her mother had decorated her to appear old enough for a baby. Four years ago, we would've glared one another down, and now I tried to look only in her eyes or not toward her at all so she couldn't tell I'd noticed the round blue earbobs sized like vanilla wafers her mother had no doubt shoved her into buying to go with the wide bangle bracelets, a necklace of blue and white painted wooden beads, thick suntan hosiery off the spinning Queen Bee rack, not pretty improvements but mean ones, temporary, and in the main so out of season it broke your heart in a million pieces on the floor by her bad-looking, wee-heeled vinyl shoes.

It hadn't occurred to me until right then that people in the same family weren't automatically in the same category of basic life culture and taste. The comedies feature stories about the poor relations, and there's Daisy Miller not knowing how to act, but in thorough realism, every atom of my aunt was so distant from my mother, I would've bet Harvard that the papers on Laura's knees had to do with the discovery that my mother had been adopted and her parents were alive very elegantly somewhere and wanting badly to meet me.

Laura tried to speak but my aunt couldn't let it happen yet, saying, Is that the same haircut you had before, Ellen? You wouldn't hear it as a trap set by someone who wanted me to fear I was funny-looking, which I knew I wasn't, not because Stuart said I wasn't but because lately I was washing my hair. I looked up and said, Oh, I'm turning out in the face. Having a maldeformed feature or being overall, vaguely ugly was something I'd avoided, a large piece of good fortune and rare. So I happened to be feeling confident with the bone structure and clear skin genes my mother had passed to me when my aunt added how lucky Laura was that my modesty over the accumulating accomplishments meant she didn't have to find bigger and bigger bowls to whack around each time I had my hair cut. Then she said, Ellen's always run her part down the middle and wouldn't listen to what it looked like.

Laura said, Ellen's not here to be spoken to like this. I'd ask you to simply say what you mean to say, but I don't see that happening, so these papers can do the talking now.

While Laura opened the folder and leaned over to separate the papers into piles on the floor in front of us, and Starletta's mother mumbled about the gall it took to give a running commentary on somebody, like they were owned, I remembered how John and Yoko protesting in bed had set my aunt off nonstop to where she couldn't drive and see a person in wire-rimmed glasses without threatening to run them down with the car. She ridiculed intellectual ideas and curiosity and felt better when people and things around her were mediocre. If you held your head up around her, you risked being made to feel beaten down or smothered, so different from the way Laura stood laughing in my door, not long before, holding books that had just arrived for the next set of weekend classes, saying, Theory of the Leisure Class and Growing Up Absurd, that's definitely us!

Bending over with Laura as she arranged the papers, I said, I should've admitted this before, but I part my hair in the middle because people with just a few brains have to do that to keep their balance.

Sitting up, she said, Do what?

Aunt Nadine, I said, tell Laura how hippies like John Lennon have to do the same thing.

When my aunt said, Ellen, that was just a manner of speaking, not something I meant, Dora said, Yes it was and still is, far as I can tell.

Dora could tell the truth on her mother, you could tell by the way she'd lifted her eyes and looked forward, because she understood her mother's meanness wasn't the theme of this room.

Laura said, Thanks, and now Nadine,

I don't know you, so I can't judge whether what you've done comes with any kind of pleasure, although I'd imagine it was worrying about everybody in this community finding out and the pain that would cause has a great deal to do with moving to Texas. At least, that's what the rumor mill's grinding out. But from what Ellen's lawyer told me this morning, another mill's been grinding, slowly as it always does and exceedingly small.

When I asked Laura what she meant, she said, Something I remember from school, I'll tell you later.

No, I said, I know it's a symbol, but what's it been grinding?

Laura said she'd thought she'd known where to start, but things were sounding disorderly already, and Dora said directly to me, You know how so much bad happened to you, and some of it just happened and some of it people did? Well, you have things coming to you from then, have had things, and you could take and put a bucket for it to all grind into, I think is how she meant it.

My aunt began jabbing her eyes with a tissue, saying, Nobody's going to want to talk about how hard losing Shine was on me when everybody tries to make me out greedy.

Laura said, I'm willing to do that. We'll say you did what you did because of grief. I'll even ignore the fact that a grown woman losing a sister doesn't compare to Ellen going without her mother, and I won't mention how she's yet to develop any kind of mean-spirited plot or raged out at anybody because of it. She's been healing and going forward, and I don't see as you've stepped a foot out of the past. But I have to know this, before the lawyer brought your atten-tion to it, did you think passing your daughter off as Ellen, introducing her to the president of a large bank, having her sign documents, did you think Ellen being there in the house and not able to save a woman determined to die from dying, did you think that entitled you to create a lie to take it all? Did you start talking about it on this road to try and get ahead of us finding out? I'd hate to have a daughter have to live with a mother who had to spend all the time and worry it must've taken to maintain the grip on that kind of hard knot.

Dora said, It kept her fairly occupied, and I said I may as well get something of my own going on, so I started dating some. But you know, I told her a thousand times I didn't want to go to jail, and she'd say I wouldn't on account of I was underage, and flip a quarter, and I'm headed to Texas, to the other side of the family I don't know anywhere well enough to walk in the door and have a baby with.

Laura said, I don't know why, but I assumed you'd be shy.

Probably, Dora said, on account of I hadn't talked to you before now.

And yes, Laura said, and so, where do you want to move?

I braced for her mother to shout rather than have Dora expose her desire to follow wither the circus band xylophone player who fathered her child went, but she excused herself to the bathroom, not to hear Dora say, This nice house on this nice street in Washington DC where this person just left to live and said I could come up there with the baby and see how it went. You have to be sixteen is the only thing hindering, and I turn that in two weeks, but Mama tries to say they don't make trains in Texas, like I'm going to follow behind her like a zombie and believe it, when she knows I used to only behave like I trusted her. Since I found out how she rooked Ellen, I can't act. But Ellen, don't think I'm trying to borrow from you because I may not be as set-set, but with what I have in mind to do, I and the baby are set.

Through the ringing that whined up in my ears, I heard my aunt in the back hall, inviting herself in to take a look at

Starletta's playthings, making herself absent from the scene of Dora getting up to narrate through the papers Laura began showing me. Starletta's mother cried out laughing about how she was going to move onto our sofa bed and let our new uniform maid bring her sandwiches. I'll say, I don't want any of it, I'd like to enjoy being a little to the side of it, but I've got to find a cleaning replacement who loves bleaching grout as much as Ellen. This was quick. I expected a stream of ridiculousness before things came to what the matter is.

When I understood the matters well enough for the time, I told Laura I needed a minute off and asked to see who else was parched. She and Dora went to the kitchen, and Starletta's mother and I walked into my room and found Starletta coloring in the Mamie Eisenhower chair with my aunt, sitting on the arm, holding the box of crayons opened down for her and saying barely to be heard, You and I'll sharpen these

before we're through. Then she looked
at me and said no louder, I couldn't
stand for you to accuse me now, so
please, if you wouldn't. I didn't take,
Ellen, but I know I kept and everything
I kept would've been your mother's. I
want her, and I despise it with her gone.
I hated people to love her. She'd loved
them back with what I needed, so when
I saw a way to keep something of her, I
did, but it's there now and yours. Nothing was wasted, the worth's become
more, so maybe you can do what I
couldn't and have it mean something to
you. I can't see that anything matters
without Shine. Do you see?

Oh, I see, I told her. I know about
scrounging for something else to feel
like it matters.

Going to pick up Starletta, her
mother said, Excuse me, I understand
why you kept all the money and land,
but it was Ellen's by law, and you got
caught and made to hand it over. You
both know Shine would say she's still

owed because you took so much other, and anybody with a soul and sense would say, Ellen, is there anything I can give you or do for you after all this, now?

Ellen knows I'd do anything, she said.

No, I don't, I told her. Nothing's expected from whom nothing was given.

Whew, it was time, Starletta's mother said, waiting for me to follow her back down the hall, for a fresh motto, healthy, wealthy, and wise.

It was also time for my cousin and me to have a way to say what was possible for us to have now between us. She made me let her carry the box to the steps, and after she set it down, she said, That's done. I'm glad, and Ellen, you may not remember, but I always enjoyed being around you and your mother. She was kind. Mine wouldn't be like she is if she could be different. Okay, well I need to get on. I'll see you again soon though. Don't you think?

Yes, I said, and it'll be something to

look forward to next time, without all this other.

When I put my arms around her, I thought we'd mash in together, not realizing how hard an eight-month stomach is and not expecting the quick, rounded knot I felt traveling across my skin. A knee, she said, or foot. So, see you next time.

And until then, I told her, remember the Alamo and you'll be fine. How could you not be? Mother of God, you've actually got a being in there, waiting, Dora, playing around.

Twelve

WHEN MY AUNT AND COUSIN LEFT, Starletta's mother lay down on the sofa and asked to hear the story in a sane, slow way now that Dora wasn't there to jump in to point out things she didn't want me to miss, like how much income the farmland around my parents' house had made each year. I was headed toward my room with Starletta and the box, but sent her on and listened. A lawyer had called Laura this morning, saying to come to his office so he could explain everything to her.

And the first thing the man said to you was what? Starletta's mother said.

Please don't get me disbarred, Laura said, smiling. He'd grown up in town, an old family, another world, gone to Harvard, come home eager to please. Ellen's grandmother's estate was the first one of any size he handled alone, and even though he thought Nadine was a crackpot for not having her mother's lawyer handle it, things flowed, things were divided, Dora signed Ellen's name where she was told and didn't appear capable of much else besides nagging her mother. When Ellen wrote the letter to Harvard, to Dr. Bok, who ran the law school before he became president, Dr. Bok called asking if he'd heard of this local go-getter named Ellen Foster who's broke and wants to start college early. He said he'd read one of Ellen's columns she'd sent along with her letter, as well as her picture from when she won the speaking event in Washington. After he called the lawyer, he phoned up Nadine.

As I was sensing the wad of confusion Dr. Bok probably felt that told him the trouble I'd declared over was actually cranked open and definitely to be avoided, Starletta's mother said, Nadine could've gotten on with the Republicans to break into the Watergate.

I know, Laura said, it doesn't seem possible, but she blindsided the young man and rolled over him. He was still edgy this morning.

But did he phone up Harvard, I asked, and make things right or was he afraid of looking like a criminal fool?

Laura said, Oh, I'm sorry, I'd meant to say, yes, he did, and he needs to see us as soon as he can get your aunt's end of things straightened out. Needless to say, all the documents need to be re-drawn, and some decisions have to be made about your aunt.

Let her go, Starletta's mother said. With the light on things here, this end is fine, and Texas is large enough to make her feel small as she needs to, and then she can be decent with the baby and allow her daughter to feel what it would've been like to have a human raise her.

When I said I hope things ended or began like that, Laura said, Don't you think it has to, with everything moving in a direction? We'll find something to lay out for supper if you want to take the box on to go through it.

An inventory among the papers had said everything else was in my grand-mother's house, and the keys for that, my old house, and a dozen tenancies were with the lawyer now, so I could go anytime and take anything out and handle it. Even though what had been in our four rooms could've fit in the box if Dora had wedged things in right, what had been in my grandmother's house would've made a sizeable grocery store feel crammed, all the shelves filled with silver, crystal, tapestry, gold. Though part of me wanted to hog it, I saw my grandmother glaring over the plates we ate countless individual chickens or turkeys on, determined I was going to break one, determined she could will me not to. I didn't think I loved her, I liked her the way you do old ladies, hard-crazed by loss, who guard their magnificent stuff in a book, and before I closed my door with the box and Starletta resting on the bed now, I called down through the house, telling Laura, You could be serving supper on gold dishes here directly if you can carry me to the big house to get some of, well, my booty.

Starletta had fallen asleep in the middle of the opened carry-around town I kept in my closet for her to play with. In the category of the giant weatherman and car salesman, I think she believed it was the one from her house with the missing traffic cop and grocer somehow present, like they lived in my closet when she went away. It was so pleasant and truthful a thought of her gorgeous double-underweared self that it would've taken more than I had, in light of the day, not to lie down by her and haul heaving, weeping for everything I didn't have but I did now, saying it was certainly sufficient, fine, filled, enough, before I opened the box.

Dora had taken care to use blue tissue and leave the lightest things for last. Moving the paper aside, I saw a yellowed Western Union message addressed to my mother at Bay View Apartments in San Francisco. Thirty-two years before, he'd said the words aloud for someone to type, and he sounded kind when he'd spoken

My dear Shine. Stop. Meet me at base Sun. noon with clean civ shirt. Stop. Make res. at Cliff House our table. Stop. Hawaii a wonder but so is my darling wife. Stop. Your loving husband.

Starletta had opened her eyes and sat up as I was reading. I said, I'm sorry. You needed to rest. Your mother and Laura are cooking, and I know they're talking about what happened at school. We've had a red-letter day, evermore one, but Mother of God, Starletta, look at those.

I reached a double strand of pearls over her head and read a note from a report card underneath them, where the teacher wrote, Ellen knows what to do and does it, a joy to teach, and my mother's answer in a Palmer penmanship hand, Ellen is smart at home as well and I admire how hard she tries with her lessons. Can we please speak sometime on whether to be concerned about too many cartoons?

I found the gold compact wrapped inside an embroidered pillowcase, and after we'd opened and closed it a few times with it up to Starletta's ear for the snap, I gave it to her to handle and

looked through tat-work aprons and an-
timacassars, the Girl Scout uniform
from when I was living with my father
and tried to be organized until it seemed
too lonesome and embarrassing after a
couple of weeks, a yellow cashmere
sweater with hazy flowers my mother
didn't wear because it was too nice,
prickled through now with holes, and a
red tin cash register I didn't remember.
Dora had taped a note on the back,

Hey Ellen,
You'll need one bigger than this
one. Ha ha. But serious, beware
not to flash what's in there in front
of my mother or you'll draw back
a nub. I'll send you where we are
so you can tell me if you think
Oscar and Maybelle sound like
names for just dogs and help me
think of names maybe out of
books as well as the best way to
leave where I am, a funny feeling
to have before you get to some-

where. Okay, just wanted to slip this in since I'm by myself for a minute. You won't believe it but best wishes always from your cousin.

The long October scarve I'd wanted was folded inside another layer of blue tissue, the last thing before some typed papers I set aside for Laura to put with the others. Unfurling it across the bed, I found a brass or gold lipstick holder, with a scene of a lady stepping up into a carriage circled around it, etched it felt. It was missing the tube of red with the white wax circle of what had tasted like a menthol medication when I took it out of her purse and put it on and when I used it, the last time, before we left the house for the funeral. Maybe it melted during a summer, while it was stored, I didn't know, but I couldn't let it stay empty or wait, so I tried the tube of coral Laura gave me. When it fit, Starletta sighed, relieved, and handed me the scarf, which I hadn't remembered being dark gold velvet on one side with the fall leaves against black silk on the other. I said aloud, But it is, and then wrapped it around the head that had dipped down to smell and touch and sympathize, I believed, saying, She carpe diems extremely and it's fine.

While I was removing some rusted pins from the padded tomato wrist cushion my mother wore when she sewed, I asked Starletta if she thought it was right that a bracelet that favored a Girl Scout craft project was the height of flair for jewelry my mother felt was good enough for her. When I said I hadn't known how little it had taken to make my mother ashamed, I waited for her to look at me with the intent to say maybe all the changes would help give me the oomph I needed to begin remembering without always slipping under the surface and reliving. I had to hear it from somebody, and she was capable, although I mostly heard her through her eyes that would open wide enough and fix on me as long as it took to believe she'd just cored down into the truth. But she was overly involved with pushing all the rings she'd found in the cash register drawers onto her fingers, thinking, I knew, that they were hers from the fair, not knowing several were real and that the rest had come from the Buster Brown chest at the shoe store.

She'd filled her fingers by scooping across the top of the drawer, so three weighted, real rings were still there, a gold band with a deep blue sapphire between two diamonds, a rectangular diamond on a gold band that I put on, remembering how it had looked too heavy for her, like something a business-woman would wear. She'd worn the diamond with the plain, slim band I found, but they didn't amount to jewelry because even the mother of the family that ate off records wore an engagement diamond and wedding band. I put them in a box on my dresser, but

I decided to wear the sapphire, telling Starletta, I think this is what I do now, you would, so there, and tell me if this doesn't look like a woman of means' hand now.

I picked up the folder and told her to come with me to leave it with the others and set the supper table. Halfway down the hall, she kept going but I called out I'd eat later and they'd understand a need for some time alone. Laura shouted over the loud frying, We know where you're coming from, just decided Starletta's going to stay home with her mother, no school, no big goon, not another minute alone, so have at it, sympathizing. You okay? Do I need to come see about something wrong with the box?

I said she didn't need to come and not to worry if she saw the door closed against the noise drifting back, just trying to be still on one of those days that called for it. When I opened the folder, I'd seen a date stamped in red beside the name and address of the state mental hospital, not a quiet, expensive one like Holden's parents would've put him in. We didn't have those, so poor or rich, you went to Dorothea Dix, a place named for a social crusader who would've shut it down if she'd been around to read the paper. If you'd read a story about the hospital, you wouldn't have needed the picture they always used of the high-spired, red brick building with the narrow, tall, barred windows to visualize what had to be happening inside, groaning, gnashing, bloodcurdling screams coming from people locked in and tormented out of their individualities and eventually released, after maddening years, into the world as zombies.

They were her admission papers, a kind of story to summarize her life and why her sister had brought her there. Looking at the date she entered and left, I couldn't remember a time when she'd been deadened in the spirit or walking dead, like the patients I'd imagined there. She was sad but there were things to be sad about, my father, her heart, the certainty that had set in with promises that nothing could change. And then the date, the tenth of September, six months before she died, said she'd missed October, spent it inside, and what pity I felt for her family since my aunt left, was gone.

She was too modest to be grouped on a ward that I'd heard they organized by the county you hail from, not your ability to get along or illness. All I knew then about her as a girl was that she wouldn't allow the maid to collect her personal laundry, and she washed her things with chamomile soap, hung them on a rack she pulled a shy curtain around, and then pressed them before she laid them back in her dresser by lavender sachets. I remembered days when I got home from school and she wasn't there, when Starletta's mother would be there to walk me across the yard and explain how everything was fine, she'd gone to the doctor and he said she'd feel better after a few days in the hospital, that's all, and she would've packed a grocery sack with clothes to spend the night at her house.

These dates said she'd been away for five weeks, and thinking back through pictures of old afternoons, the sensation of falling into a particularly deep hole came back. The only means of climbing out was the voice I heard in the story I'd lay on my bed with, a woman talking to my mother with a patient kindness to let her know, to let me know now, everything was well. Hearing the woman, it wasn't surprising days afterward when I saw among other papers a bill marked paid by my grandmother for the private room with private bath and fenced terrace she'd arranged for my mother, who'd come for rest and had hell enough in her own room with her husband at home. Despite weeks of rest, time with her that felt stretched forward to infinite then I saw now as a timeline

with the arrow replaced by an absolute
stop. We'd gathered almost everything
we were going to, and I hadn't known,

The patient presented as a frail, neatly
dressed white female, with attractive
regular features, and introduced herself
simply as Shine. By turns despondent
and hysterical throughout the
interview, she was sometimes confused
and delayed with her responses, but she
was not delusional. Her chief
complaints were fatigue and
depression. She responded slowly and
deliberately, frequently crying. She
asked and was allowed to lie down
and rest.

    She was referred for evaluation by
her primary care physician, who
expressed concern—see attached
document—that her general lethargy
would postpone the open-heart surgery
indicated by her last cardiac
examination. He recommends that staff
use the broadest possible admissions

criteria—her spouse's inability to comprehend the critical nature of both her mental and physical condition is, in his opinion, endangering her life. During her absence from the home, he will continue his ongoing discussions with the husband about obtaining inpatient treatment for his alcoholism from the Veterans Administration.

The patient expressed severe anxieties about the impending heart surgery, though she denied her fears are in any way related to the fact that the procedure is innovative and invasive. She doubts her ability to survive her recovery. When questioned, she said she is terrified that when she visualizes her nine-year-old daughter playing in the yard next summer, she does not see herself sitting on the steps to their house, watching her.

She repeatedly said that if she could only get stronger, she could be there, but she feels herself getting increasingly weaker, with physical sensations of wasting away until nothing is left of her. The patient is convinced of her worthlessness as a parent and rebuked gentle suggestions that her views may be tainted by her current depression. She is afraid that she will soon be debilitated to the extent that she will not be able to care for her daughter, recounting detailed, imaginative fears of the child starving with a mother nearby but unable to prepare a nourishing meal.

She was brought to the hospital by her mother and sister. When told that the patient was being admitted to a ward rather than a private room, both women became combative and verbally abusive. They said the patient was from a quality family and threatened to file a complaint even after it was explained that her risk for suicide would increase if she were left alone. The patient asked them to be quiet or go home, at which time they left the patient's bags and departed, again threatening legal action if the hospital allowed other patients to steal or destroy their contents.

The patient calmed considerably. After standing to say good-bye to them, she asked to remain lying down during the remainder of the intake and frequently apologized for being exhausted. When told that her latest cardiac tests showed adequate justification for her complaint, she insisted it was her own fault. Nursing staff interrupted intake at 11:40 to record vitals, which were sent to the medical department for preparation of her chart.

The patient began asking repeatedly after the care of her daughter during her hospitalization and was reminded that the girl would be cared for by her sister. When she was offered assurance that her husband was at home for additional immediate support of the child and that her physician was seeing to her husband's own recovery, she became hysterical. She was administered .5 mg. Valium PO.

She responded to the proverbs as follows:

Spilt milk—Don't cry over things that aren't real.

Thrown stones and glass houses—Be more at home, and try to keep it neat. You should live in a brick house if possible. It can't come down. But why would I throw a stone in my house? I wouldn't do that. I didn't.

Wolves in sheep's clothing—You can't get help from the wolves if you don't have any power. You have to have money to have power. I used to be rich. If I were a wolf, I could get rid of him. It wouldn't matter what clothes I was wearing. My mother buys Liberty fabrics for my daughter's little dresses. Did I tell you that?

Rolling stone and moss—Don't be irresponsible. If you're forced to roll, you could scrape off the moss. Clean up the mess you made. I made a mess of my life. Did I tell you that?

When asked about her home life, she said she wasn't lonely, that her daughter frequently stays in bed with her, coloring and playing school. When asked to describe a recent occurrence that brought her pleasure, she said it was watching Ed Sullivan with her daughter, who surprised her by singing along all the words to a song. She became distraught and could not continue. The interview was halted while she rested and was administered oxygen, after which she appeared more comfortable.

When further questioned about her family, she said she worshipped her child but was terrified that life was getting away from her. She said she'd made a deal with the devil when she married her husband, who seemed determined not to let either of them have a long and happy life. When asked to explain, she said she married him to get away from home and have the excitement her parents had shielded her from, although she described her adolescent years as lovely and very happy.

She said he was clever and good-looking, so she was incredulous that he was attracted to her. She described his family as being well-off enough but hard-living, and though she initially enjoyed the fact that he didn't treat her with kid gloves and didn't make concessions to her often delicate health, his coarse treatment of her escalated as her health declined.

The key events in her marriage were the birth of her child and the death of her husband's father, which occurred in the same year. She said her husband lost his way permanently at that time and began drinking continuously. Not only does he miss his father's direction, he misses the time he spent on an aircraft carrier in the Pacific, she said, and often seems to live in the past and regret that nothing as exciting has happened to him since.

She became inaudible, saying she had to admit something terrible and embarrassing. The night before, her husband had broken a lamp on top of the television because a program with the actor Robert Stack was on. She said he stays livid with the actor because they were on the same crew aboard the ship and the man has done considerably better. When asked if the child witnessed the violence and if she has ever witnessed such an outburst, the patient rolled over and faced the wall, saying nobody would believe it if they were told.

When asked if the child needed to be removed from the home before her mother and sister could collect her, she said her husband actually idolized the child in his own way and is counting on her to live out his old dream of an exciting life. She said he was too lazy to take advantage of the GI Bill yet sees himself as a neglected grand man.

She asked the staff's opinion on the question of what would happen to her daughter if something happened to her and then answered that people would know her husband was unfit and would remove her and raise her correctly. She says she will keep pressing her family for forgiveness for marrying someone they despised and putting herself in such a dangerous position and hopes they will, in turn, care for her child. Hysterical again, she said the child would suffer whether she lived or died, and she felt tortured by the embarrassment of having a child look up to a mother who wouldn't defend herself and let them live at the mercy of a cruel and negligent man.

Note that a message was forwarded

to the North Ward desk at 12:10 recommending that her 15-minute suicide checks be elevated to constant watch for at least the next 72 hours.

She claimed no support from her husband and said he makes her afraid by overdrawing their accounts at the bank, and part of her feelings of worthlessness involve a dire sense of having deprived her daughter of things and said if the child didn't have the bookmobile and TV, she'd have nothing at all. She said her husband humiliates her by saying she lived well enough as a child to last all her life and seems unconcerned that the lack of air-conditioning and physical labor required in a rural home, for example, make her heart condition worse.

She produced five one-hundred-dollar bills from her dress pocket, saying her mother had given the money to her that morning and told her to use it for an escape, but she was too tired and asked the staff to keep it

locked away from her husband should
he arrive. Her mother, said she, put ten
thousand dollars on deposit for the
child's education when she was born,
but her husband took the money and
she is still too afraid to ask where it
has gone.

When asked if she had ever
considered divorce, she said she was
too miserable and weak to go through
it and would not know how to be a
person without a home and a husband
to care for. She claimed to love her
husband, although her affect was flat
when she spoke of him.

Her childhood background was
marked by the onset of scarlet fever at
five years old with a resultant
rheumatic fever, which led to her
coronary debilitation. Her father was
her primary caregiver as her mother
was too impatient. He named her
Shine, she said, because she sang at the
table. He gave her a new car for her
last birthday at home and also for

completing school with a perfect academic and attendance record. She said he set an example with his lovely manners, and then she said he died during her fourth year of marriage, at which time she asked for a cup of water.

She left a teachers college before the end of her first semester and moved to Alameda, California, and worked as a secretary at a shipyard while her husband was in the Pacific. She said they were married on the steps of a courthouse in San Francisco with many other couples. When asked if this was a pleasant time, she said she had a nice, neat kitchen and went out with other wives and listened to music, had tea at a nice hotel, and sunbathed on the cliffs sometimes but since arriving home twenty-five years ago, she hasn't really done anything social.

She says she enjoys her neighbors but can't have them in her home and going to theirs has become too sad.

When her mother or sister take her for medical appointments, they take her shopping, although she has to remove tags so her husband will not cash in the purchases.

She was well-mannered at all times and brightened when describing her daughter as a kind and funny child who seems oddly precocious. Her daughter has been real rather than play help, she said. She learned to walk holding a broom.

Her weight, 98 pounds, was attributed to eating nothing but cookies and cakes when her child is in bed with her sometimes on days she can't get up, which are becoming more frequent, as are fainting spells and attacks of neuralgia.

When questioned about the two fainting spells her sister reported her as having in a single week she said she'd wanted to finish cooking without her daughter knowing so she could stay outdoors with a friend. Crying again, she asked that the staff not tell her child that she'd fainted and was an inadequate parent. She claimed to have several acquaintances who could come by and help, but she is ashamed to admit she needs help when she brought the problem on herself.

Her daughter, she said, gave her what she needed inside, although she said she didn't know what she would do if the fear and despair became larger than the love she felt for her child. She then became nonresponsive and moderately catatonic in affect.

She signed the documents with difficulty but legibly and was admitted for a recommended six-week course of treatment for major depression and anxiety. Before leaving the area, she asked when she would be allowed to rest again and expressed fear of being around loud and out-of-control people.

She was administered .25 mg. Navane BID and placed in a wheelchair. Her person and personal possessions were searched with staff present to witness.

Removed from her purse—One gold mirror compact—One nail clipper—Driver's license—Social Security card—child and patient's eye and dental appt. cards—One small glass frame—envelope addressed to patient containing twenty one-hundred-dollar bills, typewritten hotel reservation for mother and child, train confirmation to Warm Springs, instructions for leaving area upon discharge, letter of credit, from office of pres., Providential Bank—child's school picture removed and placed in her pocket with one red Chap Stick—Gold case removed. Money, Items to be secured. Will call sister re appt. cards—call bank re courier delivery of envelope contents.

Removed from her person—One bottle Digitalis, 100 mg./50 prescribed to patient—One bottle Valium, .5 mg./40 prescribed to patient's sister—One matchbox containing 20 ct.

yellow pellets, assumed to be a household poison.

Listen to her, shivering desperate, with poison in her pocket and the means for us to go to a place that sounded comfortable, far, and serene.

It was dark outside now, and everything that had happened since the sun came up that morning accumulated and wouldn't be swallowed down, and though it was Monday, it felt like Sunday evening, too late to begin anything, too soon to end, willfully holding back hours from passing, frustrating you out of going and doing. I sat at my desk with the papers, thinking, Little wonder she killed herself between Sunday and Monday.

When I looked in my dresser mirror, I looked chaotic in the face. I'd forgotten how quickly order flies off the rail until Laura opened the door and I told her, It needs to stop being Sunday. You think I can afford to pay it to be gone?

I swear before God, all I want to buy is a shearling coat and time.

She took the papers and looked through them, sighing and moving me with her, saying, The fireplace, we were throwing cloves on it to kill a burn smell. Sit by it and let me look at these, what, admission records?

Yes, I said, but the last page is it. It's it.

Folding a blanket narrowly away from the fire, she sat on the floor in front of Starletta and her mother arranged on the sofa, I told them, like a birthing. I didn't ask whether anybody realized how convenient it was that they were both available to shape themselves into a simile. I asked, Did anybody know my mother and had I the means to go to a place called Warm Springs? Can you see the connotations and all the routine chances we missed? And now I can get a charge out of knowing we almost made a narrow escape to somewhere that favored the atmosphere this room would have in it right now if I wasn't spending all the power of positive thinking here on not coming apart. And let me tell you about this other. You know how I enjoy irony? Well, I'm having some kind of time knowing I've been miserable since she died because she died so I wouldn't be miserable. She thought she was a failure to me because she couldn't go and do like most, and it was already almost more than you could bear if you woke up first and saw her. I didn't know she was going around needing her hands occupied to stop her from killing herself or I would've made sure they were taken, you know, all the time.

Starletta's mother turned on her side and said, You couldn't tell what was on her mind by any means you used to try. If she'd lived toward this house and Laura had known she was sad or tired, she would've been offered a bed of nice linens and tea on the tray, but nobody guessed how bad she felt and helpless to reverse it. If you'd known, you and she would be at the other end of the sofa with us.

Looking at Starletta's wrap head, I felt myself envy the way she knew what made her happy and did it regardless of the day or hour. She didn't stoop in the doors of little houses, examining, and she didn't have a catalog of poems on life passing her by or a state of panicked absence to crawl in when she missed her mother, she darted into rooms until she found her. I watched her while I listened to her mother say I was lucky to have money to throw at my problems. Although money hadn't solved the girlhood woes of her inspiration, Madame C. J. Walker, she'd built a mansion to live in while she was trying. The women, she said, who live on in time, lived inside their time and did with it. They didn't believe waiting pertained to them and wore the second set of pants when they had to.

She would've crawled in the fire if she

believed it was necessary for Starletta to be happy, and I saw what my mother had done had nothing to do with anything but one woman's ability to believe deeply and allow passions, convictions, truth, nothing watered down, and to love so enormously that the space would naturally be as large. My mother's love was what I was made of, and I'd been filled already, never endured a time when I wasn't, but I didn't feel it until I understood that she intended to die, and she intended to feel her love present, not remembered like something missing that I had to stay scrambling to have back. Laura called me to come over to where she was on the floor and show her the ring, her arms and legs already opened, listening to me saying the ring had been hers, telling me, I know, I know, and I love you, I know.

Christmas Eve
1975

IF YOU LIVE IN A TEMPERATE CLI-
mate, I hope you awaken to snow. If
you live in a continuous frozen zone, I
trust you're enjoying a sturdy igloo and
kind people to share it with, and if
you're in a tropical locale, I expect
you've accumulated some imagination,
and things such as spray snow for your
Christmas tree and bulk cotton balls for
tabletop displays of cheery scenes of
winter.

No matter where you're living, I hope you sleep peacefully tonight and waken into relief, not so hounded by worry you miss listening for the reindeer feet, even if you've grown older, as I have, and depend on memories of thrilling wishes. With no regrets or grudges against the tin and timber real life around you, let it be time to bring every memory inside like wood you place in the fireplace piece by piece, wish by wish. The old need that wasn't met, the wants misunderstood, what you absolutely knew and guessed, what you dreamed or half invented, saw and heard outright or saw and heard in words you read and adored, what was done to you and calls for revenge you let burn away. Each thing is of the same good use, and burning together, continually, the light the bundle makes belongs to you, your love and work, what you see by, how you're seen. By December, I understood the deeper the dreams and beliefs, the brighter and warmer you and the rooms

you walk through are, and you're safe
now passing through old places, not
dark now, more than sufficiently kept lit
by you.

Late in the afternoon on Christmas
Eve, I answered when Starletta's mother
called just before we left for her house to
be sure we weren't bringing anything besides, she said, the set of sheets you'll
need to sleep on the sofa pulled out and
scissors. Mine, I've yet to find from un-
packing. Oh, and you know the low
shoe shelf in your mother's closet that
things like to roll across the slope of the
floor and be under? Bringing tape would
save me from having to get on my hands
and knees with clean clothing on or
sending Starletta in to investigate. Hold
on for me to think, yes, we just needed
a safety pin for something, the clasp on
her Rudolph's broken.

When I said it sounded like they were
making a Halloween costume, she said,
It feels like ten years went through my
body, and the mind's following.

I said, I know. I'm still sorry it wasn't as easy as it sounded to get you into my old house and my friend from his sinking one into yours. If it weren't for Stuart, we'd still be hauling the family of four's leavings hither and yon.

I've never seen anybody as proud as he was to offer a pile of burning rubber to us, she said. He rode by yesterday and fixed a cold window for me, where the new seal fell out, and Martha rode by this morning with several very pretty things for Starletta, saying she's able to watch her for the classes I need at night now, and then days through the summer. So when you're around, you and she can take her to the city pool, movies, and so forth.

I know, I said, and Luther talked to Martha's mother and got on at the store. When I met him in the pasture this morning to trade gifts, he asked if taxidermy work qualified him for a promotion behind the meat counter.

She said, Where I got these livers I'm

doing my thing with here, and Starletta's doing her thing, plugging in lights, cracking nuts, what have you. Is your mother about ready? Oh, but tell her I don't need her old fireplace screen. After the masons finished, they accidentally hid the screen and poker setup behind Shine's garden shelter for Starletta to find and turn into a playhouse.

You know, I said, I could get the veteran to build her something like Mrs. Tom Thumb lives in at the fair. A miniature house has her number all over it. When we get there, I'll wrap one of the houses from her carry-around town, and don't say it's too much or coming from not having a place to bake mud when I was little. I'd do it for the charge of watching her set up housekeeping.

Laura had come in to stand, listening, and then she took the phone and said, The landlady and I will be over there directly. If I were you and trying to study and keep Starletta occupied, I'd be mixing concrete instead of batter. Remember the day you pulled her out of school, when you came over for us to think and then had so much other happen? Well, regard it like Ellen's making good on the ideas I've owed you and see if that takes the edge off getting a present on Christmas.

As Laura and I came around a curve and saw the bridge, where the road straightens toward what everyone was easily calling Starletta and her mother's new house, we slowed to see how much closer Marvin's old house was to floating off and agreed with others who'd begun slowing or stopping on the bridge for the same reason, thinking, Whew, just in time. Even though Marvin and his father were going to be cooking something they'd shot and opening gifts they'd carved by the tree they'd cut down and still so choked up by their new home they probably wouldn't be able to make a great deal of sense talking, we turned down Starletta's old path with their gifts, an electric shaver chosen for the father because he needed one and a pop-up toaster for Marvin, for how staggered he'd been the morning he came to pick up the house keys from us and learned Pop-Tarts were invented to be eaten hot.

They weren't at home, and no dogs barked, so I left the things on the steps for them to find when they returned from hunting and told Laura, They can snack and groom before supper at least, let's roll on.

The family of four was confused and unwilling to ignore the infinite lease my aunt had given them so she could think less and less about the house and what happened there, but they dashed with little more than the clothes on their backs when the lawyer made them the offer I said they couldn't refuse on account it involved moving to the verge of town, where houses start being closer together in rows. Laura and I knew they'd be ambitious for one of the split-level rentals on the scraped orange clay lots.

Their house looked beaten down in a hot hurry though, which said they'd settled in well and were living out their human nature, dirtier but no different at heart from what Marvin and his father, Starletta and her mother, and Laura and I were trying to do. Organizing them out of my old house was important to help keep chaos down after decisions exploded toward us, although the action cooled as my aunt and cousin straightened their end out in Texas and began doting on the baby, a girl, seven pounds, named Claire Ellen.

When Laura called to make our first appointment, the lawyer told her things didn't get this unfamiliar and he'd meet with us at home as much as possible. He came that afternoon, and as we watched him going through his satchel on the hood of his car, a diesel, Laura said, He's young but if I could start over at twenty or so, I'd go for that, expensive, studious, rangy-boned.

Narrow-assted, I said, is what Faulkner would call his shape in the hips. And now's not the time to ask and you don't need to tell me, but why didn't you get married?

Because, she said, the subject never came up.

I said okay then and let the man in. After we got through the whipping he gave himself for goofing so severely, he said, Before we go forward, Dr. Bok sent a letter and asked that I give it to you and explain that the help he refers to is mine, not that I wouldn't offer it or need another job if this estate doesn't get me fired.

I don't know, Laura said, as this estate goof-up is my kind of comedy. Though I can certainly see the potential, I think Ellen's earned the right to tell it like it's funny first. Don't you think?

Oh, I said, taking the letter, unless this is Dr. Bok saying after he heard about the ordeal with my aunt, he gave my spot to Walter Mitty because he already had all the female sociopaths he could use.

While I was reading the letter, Laura took him in the kitchen, and over the sounds of her making coffee, I heard, If Ellen can't find a word for something, good or bad, it's floored her. You'll be working with her, so you should know, she's not making herself up for your benefit. I could shake her in the middle of the night and ask her what Jack the Ripper was, and she'd say, murderer, sociopath.

I heard him say, I saw a copy of the letter she sent to Harvard and wondered, as you would, about things at home, especially with the serious size of this estate she's inherited and you, as the guardian and trustee, in the most influential position to guide things. But what you just said, is that fairly typical conversation around the house?

When Laura told him she supposed people bloomed where they were planted and he didn't answer, she said, The library in there isn't wallpaper, and if it was, Ellen could've searched sample

patterns and talked to me about sociopaths simultaneously. She's happiest
doing both and requires it. Her having a
dollar in one part of her life and a million or more in the rest doesn't concern
me. What does though is how quiet she
is with the letter. It'd help if I knew.

When I was through, I took the letter to her, saying, You don't need to
strong-arm him, Laura, here,

Dear Ellen,

I've asked my friend to give you
this note, along with the enclosed
information about Harvard we've
gathered for you. He is looking
forward to helping you to continue your extraordinary achieve-
ments. He was an excellent and
memorable student, and although
I have doubted that his hometown
would offer him enough challenge
and room to grow, I am confident
you will provide him with both.

I've taken the liberty of meeting

with my colleagues here who are in charge of our admissions procedures and requirements. After reading your letter and reviewing your application and supplementary documents, we all agreed that you are Harvard material and then some. We want you to know that your place in the Class of 1981 is guaranteed. However, we want you to flourish here, and we do not believe that beginning a conventional undergraduate program at fifteen is the best means to that end.

We propose that you begin attending summer classes this year, residing in one of our women's dormitories. We hope you'll want to return for each of the following two summers before you graduate high school, and, perhaps after your senior year in high school, enroll in one of our overseas summer programs. The summer courses you take will accrue credits that will count toward graduation requirements when you enroll as a full-time student in the fall of 1977. I'm confident Harvard will be as enriched by your presence as you will be stimulated, as you so thoughtfully expressed, by the intellectual environment.

At Harvard, we're proud of our tradition of educating those most worthy, and while I am extremely pleased to hear your financial circumstances have greatly improved, we want to offer you a full scholarship. During your college years, you should not feel compelled to apply yourself to any endeavor other than expanding the already considerable scope of your mind and building your character, which is clearly unusually strong.

All the information you need to apply to this summer's program is enclosed. Please do not hesitate to call our admissions director with any questions that arise. I hope you will let me know the date of your arrival this summer. We'll leave the books behind and go on, I suppose you would say, a walking, talking tour along the river. Until then, Miss Foster, congratulations on all you've accomplished, and I greatly look forward to meeting you this summer.

Your friend,
Derek C. Bok

I told Laura, I bet I can do this, don't you think?

Saying, Think it, know it, you're here, so yes, Laura answered the same question each time we waited outside the door to my mother's old house. Stuart had reinstalled the doorknob, but I wasn't able to turn it and walk nonchalantly through yet, like the place hadn't mattered. I was still studying neglect on Christmas Eve, while we leaned against the door, holding presents and knocking with a toe. When we heard Starletta running from the front of the house, I told Laura I'd be interested to know why I felt better inside the house than waiting.

Mother of God, she shouted, Starletta's coming toward us with new blinking shoes. We can sort through leftover nerves, Ellen. Watch her, just watch that, regard her high-voltage feet!

As her mother held back the door, she said, Santa Claus decided to bring the shoes early. We needed something to set the right tone, but, Ellen, I want you to feel free to think about not spending the night. It's Starletta's long toes under her foot lights, and it's Shine's house inside all the Christmas we put around. This may not be the time yet.

I told her and Laura, Being here, if you stand right here, and just be standing, you don't have the sensation of the floorboards opening up, and I don't think the ground's going to come up at midnight and swallow the bed, but I could use another October. Maybe not. One more of those may be called for.

What I believe, Laura said, is you knowing the time's coming will work well for you, Ellen, knowing it's certain.

Being obligated to carry change and lean every element toward winter, October couldn't keep the sky waiting. It had to come before the leaves could be released, like a permission. October's slightest responsibility still had the universe hinged on it, various safeties regarding the wind and extremes of temperature that could freeze a continent or sink it. When you compare and contrast the duties you stay expected to perform because of all the outlandish gifts you were given when you were little and talents you were furnished in your womb, if you accumulated everything that's ever expected of you, they'd never amount to more than the kind of mean little pile of coins misers sit around and trick between their fingers continually, not much of a wonder of achievement at all.

It wasn't an accomplishment either, realizing I was less important than the weather, it was a red-letter event in the history of an older girl looking toward the rest of the changes due to come on like seasons, rowed like the houses along my road, turning over like plowed ground folding. That kind of occurrence would automatically have something to do with love. Laura gave me love, but my mother's spirit was the light I needed to show the way into her, and she was able to stop straining to reach me. We rested from the giving and taking and stayed still together, telling one another we could do this through any commotion, going and doing and doing it well. Knowing well that I could be more than what my mother did, more than the moment she died—I am what she was before and is now, here with me in the burden of her love I'm content to carry, gorgeous to me and lighter than breath.